SIXTY FIVE HOURS

N.R. WALKER

COPYRIGHT

65 SIXTY FIVE HOURS

N.R. WALKER

CHAPTER ONE

I SAT in my office trying not to watch him.

But I did.

His office was across from mine. The glass walls provided a daily distraction, because for the fucking life of me, I did not want to watch him.

But I did.

I didn't like him. In fact, he pissed me off. He was a gorgeous, fucking arrogant, self-righteous sonnova bitch. The boss' son. Wealthy, smart, impeccably dressed.

And straight.

The women in the office, no scratch that, in the entire building, fawned over him. It was embarrassing, really. They'd check their make-up before he walked in, they'd bat their eyelashes, giggle and flirt without shame. And he'd just smile that smug fucking smile - that gorgeous, heart-stopping smile - and left them all aflutter in his wake.

I'd been here for six months and as far as I knew, he'd never dated anyone from the office. He must have those professional-boundaries work-ethics I'd read about. Either that, or Boss-Daddy prohibited inter-office relations.

My personal assistant, Rachel, swore he was a nice guy. She was best friends with Simona, who happened to be *his* personal assistant. He smiled and chatted with both of them, but if I happened to walk past them, he'd glare at me. I acted like it didn't bother me, give the girls a grin, and a dip of an imaginary hat I obviously wasn't fucking wearing. And they loved it.

I wasn't sure if that's what pissed him off, or maybe he didn't like Texans. Maybe he didn't like the fact I was head-hunted from one of the most lucrative advertising agencies in Dallas. Maybe it was because I was given an office right across the hall from him, next to his father's. Maybe it was because I was hand-picked by his Daddy-dearest, and he was threatened I might just be better at this job than him.

Maybe he didn't like me because I'm gay.

But I didn't think that was it. He was friendly enough with Marcus, from Accounts. I'd seen them talking plenty of times and Marcus was so damn gay he made *my* head spin. Surely a creeped out homophobe wouldn't go anywhere near the poster child of lilac cashmere and lip gloss.

From the day I first met him, he'd been cold toward me. I'd flown up to Chicago for the interview for Senior Advertising Executive with the prestigious Fletcher Advertising, Inc. We met and chatted nicely for two minutes before his father came in and the informal interview started. Yes, it was informal, but still an intense interview. I was a little nervous, but I was me: professional, honest and direct.

See, the thing is, I'm very fucking good at what I do. I don't mince words, and I don't waste time. So when I was asked if I had any questions, I said, "Just one."

The two men looked at me to continue.

So, I did. "I don't need to tell you how good I am at my

job. You have my portfolio, and quite frankly, I doubt I'd be sitting here if you didn't already know that I alone can increase your account profitability by at least twenty-five percent. Hell, if I haven't reached that target within the first year, you can either kick my ass or fire it. But what is not written on my CV anywhere is that I'm gay."

Both men blinked.

"I don't advertise my sexuality, nor do I hide it. This is the *only* time I expect to discuss this matter with you, so I need to know before we waste anymore time, if you, or this company, is in anyway uncomfortable or homophobic? If the answer is yes, then I'll thank you both for the opportunity, but I'll be back in Texas in time for supper."

And with that, the boss smiled, stood and shook my hand, while the son looked like he'd just been shit on from a great height. I started two weeks later and Cameron Fletcher had been indifferent to me since.

I wouldn't say hostile. But I certainly wouldn't say pleasant, either.

A sharp rap on my door snapped me out of my memories before it opened. My suave and distinguished, Armani-suited boss stepped into my office. "Lucas?"

"Yes, Mr. Fletcher?"

"My office. Ten minutes."

"Sure." I smiled at him.

He closed the door, and I looked at Rachel for some kind of explanation. She shrugged, and we both turned back to the glass wall and watched Mr. Fletcher knock on his son's door.

"Cameron?"

He stepped inside and we could no longer hear any spoken words, but we watched the silent father and son conversation.

"He doesn't look happy," Rachel said beside me.

"Which one?" I asked.

She giggled. "Cameron."

"Is he ever happy?"

She nudged my shoulder and smiled a twisted pout at me, playfully telling me to leave him alone.

Mr. Fletcher walked out of Cameron's office, and we watched as Cameron sat at his desk, ran his hands through his hair twenty times and swung his chair around so we could no longer see him.

We watched Simona quickly sort out files and hand them to him, then Rachel said, "Shoot, Lucas! It's time. Go! Don't be late." She all but pushed me out the door, just as Cameron's door opened directly in front of me.

Ignoring Cameron completely, I tipped my invisible hat and smiled at Simona. "Miss Simona."

She grinned, and Cameron rolled his eyes and stalked off in front of me. I soon realized, he was also heading to his father's office.

Shit.

I followed him, entering through the open double doors at the end of the hall. Mr. Fletcher's office was huge; open, light and contemporary yet stylish. There was a large archer's arrow embellishing the wall behind his desk. The archer's arrow symbol, the Fletcher Advertising icon, was on the Fletcher family crest apparently.

The arrow, that simple, signature piece was on every fucking thing; doors, windows, stationary, furniture; television, internet, magazines, newspapers. That very arrow was synonymous with advertising across the country. It represented excellence in this industry.

Hell, there was even one next to my name on my business cards.

They didn't need a catch-phrase, or cheesy slogans. The symbol on its own said enough. When you saw the arrow, you thought Fletcher Advertising. Simple and effective.

Genius.

"Ah, Lucas," Mr. Fletcher, the man behind the genius, said. "Come, take a seat."

Cameron was there, though not looking at me. Truthfully, I was a little nervous as to the meaning behind this meeting and why it was just us three. Impromptu and exclusive meetings with the boss always made me tense, so I did the first thing that came naturally. I leaned back in my seat, crossed one ankle over my knee and smiled like we were there to discuss weekend football.

Smug, yeah. Cocky, maybe.

I sold advertising for fuck's sake.

It was my job to look like I knew the secret to your success.

It was an act. I knew that, but the client, the guy across the table holding the check book didn't.

"I suppose you're both wondering why I've called you in here," Mr Fletcher started, though he didn't give either of us time to speak. "I heard through the grapevine a certain lifestyle product company is in need of new marketing. I made some phone calls and have secured a one-off chance meeting to convince them they need us."

"Lurex," Cameron said confidently. "I read an article with the new CEO in Business Review USA. He said then he'd like to broaden horizons."

Mr. Fletcher nodded at his son and smiled, a little proudly. "Yes. Lurex."

Holy shit. The biggest *lifestyle product company*, as Mr. Fletcher so delicately put it, was the biggest manufacturer of condoms, personal lubricant and sex aides in the country.

That account would be... massive. Career-making kind of massive.

I could feel my grin getting wider, and Mr. Fletcher smiled when he looked at me. But it was Cameron who spoke. "Why are you telling *both* of us?"

That was a good point. I looked at Cameron then, though he still hadn't looked at me. His eyes were trained on his father.

"The meeting is 10 AM, Monday."

I blinked. I was sure Cameron blinked. Then I blinked again.

"As in three days away?" my mouth said before my brain could stop it. It was four o'clock on Friday for fuck's sake.

"Yes," Mr. Fletcher said slowly, like I was mentally handicapped. "In sixty-five hours I want Fletcher Advertising to walk into that meeting with a new product design, new target market, new campaign."

I stopped short of asking him if he'd lost his fucking mind and settled for shifting in my seat instead.

Mr. Fletcher looked at me, then at Cameron, and he said, "It's a twenty million dollar contract, and I want it. You are both exceptionally talented and, given an open schedule, I have no doubt either one of you could secure the deal."

Oh, fuck... I was pretty sure I knew where he was going with this....

"But we don't have an open schedule," Mr. Fletcher said. "We have sixty-five hours. That's why you will both work together over the weekend to make sure we walk into that meeting and blow them away."

Work together. Work all weekend.

Yep. That's what I thought.

Fuck.

Cameron tried to object, but his father stood up. The

meeting was apparently over. Mr. Fletcher walked over to the double doors that led through to the conference media room and I looked over at Cameron. He was staring at his father's now empty chair, and I imagined the look on my face wasn't much better.

"Boys!" Mr. Fletcher called out.

I was quick to follow, and Cameron wasn't far behind me. There were two brown paper grocery bags on the conference table, which Mr. Fletcher waved his hand at. "Get to know your product as it is now, what it's lacking. Turn it into something someone can't live without. I'll be in touch."

And then it was just me and Cameron. And two brown paper bags.

Sighing, I up ended one of the bags, and the contents spilled over the table. Condoms. Boxes of them. Ribbed, studded, colored, thin, long, for her pleasure, for his, you name it, it was there. Lubricants of every flavor, glitter, sparkle, self-heating, tingling....

I smiled when it occurred to me I'd tried most of these.

I peeked into the other bag and, from the corner of my eye, I noticed Cameron move. I shrugged at him. "I'm not happy about this either," I told him, handing him whatever it was I had in my hands, so I could empty the second bag.

When he looked at what I'd given him, I looked at it too, realizing I'd just handed him a box of strawberry flavored lube. He looked at the box, then at me and exhaled through puffed cheeks. I started pulling boxes out of the second bag when I realized he was re-packing the first bag.

"What are you doing?" I asked.

"I'm not doing this here," he said, a simple matter of fact.

"What?" I said too loudly. "You heard what your-"

He cut me off. "I said I'm not doing this *here*," he

repeated, clearly flustered. He pulled out a business card and his pen from his pocket, then scribbled down something before handing it to me. "It's my home address," he explained before I could ask. "If I'm going to be stuck working all weekend, then I may as well be comfortable. I'll have Simona drop off everything we need."

He looked at his watch. "I'll be home in an hour."

And just like that, I was being sequestered for the next sixty-five hours with a man who couldn't stand the sight of me.

CHAPTER TWO

I AM... NOT A FAN OF CLOCKS THAT COUNT BACKWARDS

AFTER EXPLAINING to Rachel what my new weekend plans involved and leaving her in a blur of organizational motion, I headed home to change. I packed an overnight bag of clothes, and exactly one hour after Cameron handed me his home address, I was walking up the steps to his house.

It was nice. Very fucking nice.

A newly renovated brownstone, little porch out the front, there was even a fucking tree. It was a little tree, but it was still a tree. Not many people living ten minutes from Chicago's city centre had trees in their front yards.

Not many people even had front yards.

Except for Cameron Fletcher.

Figured.

I paused before pressing the doorbell. Fucking hell. It was ten past five on Friday afternoon, and my weekend was over before it began. I'd worked plenty of weekends. And nights. But not with someone who despised me.

I sighed, mumbled, "Ah fuck it," and pressed the damn button.

He opened the door almost immediately, like he was on the other side of the door listening to me hesitate. He was still dressed in work clothes, sans the jacket. His tie was pulled down, the top button undone.

Fuck. There was no denying it. He was gorgeous. Beautiful, actually. Not really a word I use to describe men. But he was beautiful -- as tall as me, lean, hazel eyes, alabaster skin, an artfully distressed mop of coffee colored hair and the most kissable pink lips....

Yep. Beautiful.

He looked me up and down, his eyes fixing on my feet, and he coughed a little before standing aside to let me in. I looked down at my clothes; jeans, tee shirt, jacket and boots. Standard Lucas Hensley wardrobe.

If he wasn't straight, I'd think he was checking me out. It wasn't like I hadn't checked him out before, many times. I mean, he was a man, a beautiful man, and I'm a hot-blooded gay man. I'm gonna look. It's a given.

He stood there, at a loss of what to say. So I spoke instead. "So, where we gonna do this?"

"Oh," he said, "this way." And he led me through the first door off the hall. It was a living room. Very tastefully decorated, contemporary but lived in.

"Nice place," I offered.

"Yeah, thanks," he said quietly. "I love it here."

He waved his hand at the large square dining table where there were papers and files laid out with a laptop. "I've started to set up here," he explained. "But I need to get changed... kitchen's through that door." He pointed to another door. "Help yourself to whatever you want; water, beer, soda. I'll just be upstairs."

He turned and walked out the door we came through, and I called out, "You want a drink?"

He was silent for a beat, but then he yelled back, "Just water for me." Then he added, "Um, thanks."

So I grabbed us both a bottled water and sat myself at Cameron's dining table. I tried not to look around his living room. I could see photos but didn't focus on the people in them. I didn't want to be rude.

Even I could respect boundaries.

So I flipped through the files instead. I got about half way through the client summary brief on Lurex when Cameron came back downstairs. This time I did check him out.

He was only wearing jeans, a button down shirt and slip-on Italian loafers that probably cost more than my first car, but he looked... *different*.

Different, as in not in a suit, no jacket, no tie. Cameron Fletcher in designer suits was fucking easy to look at, but seeing him go casual... well, it took the term easy on the eye to a whole new level.

He cleared his throat, and I realized I'd been caught checking him out. I gave him a casual shrug, acknowledging my wandering eye, but certainly didn't apologize for it.

Embarrassed and ignoring me completely, he sat in front of his laptop and started tapping at the board. "Simona will be here soon," he said, looking fixedly at the screen in front of him.

"And Rachel," I informed him. "They were getting everything organized when I left."

He nodded and opened his mouth, but then closed it again, clearly deciding not to say whatever it was he was about to say. Then he looked at me, and said it anyway. "Have to cancel any plans this weekend?"

That was the first conversational thing he had ever said to me. I smiled and shook my head. "Nah. I've only been here six months. Not really long enough to meet anyone outside of work. You?"

His brow pinched, and he shook his head no. Again, he opened his mouth to speak, but this time was saved by the doorbell.

He got up and ten seconds later, a whiteboard with two legs walked into the room. Rachel. I jumped up quickly and took the whiteboard from her. It was taller and wider than she was with her arms outstretched – which wasn't difficult - and she had two satchels over her shoulders.

"Jeez Rach, you'll do yourself an injury," I complained.

"There's more." She nodded her head pointedly to the front door. "Go make yourself useful."

I grinned and made my way outside, passing Simona and Cameron, who had their arms full, on my way. "That should be the last of it," Simona called out over her shoulder.

Rachel and I collected the last remaining archive boxes from the trunk, closed it and headed back inside. Simona and Cameron were having some kind of silent conversation – she was looking at him with pleading in her eyes, and he shook his head and glared a flat no in his.

And I wondered if there was more to them than met the eye. They obviously had a history. I just wondered if it had ever been more than just professional. But their silent conversation stopped very deliberately when I walked in.

Cameron quickly busied himself setting the whiteboard up, and I took a look at the amount of stuff the girls brought with them. "Did you leave *anything* at the office? Or is it all here?"

Rachel smiled and then explained the two leather satchels. "Laptop, and client history on marketing and accounts."

"Don't know what I'd do without you," I said, nudging her with my elbow.

"You'd have brought all this shit here on your own, that's what you'd do without me," she quipped back at me then she bumped her hip into mine. "But thanks for saying it."

I spied the two bags of Lurex goodies and realized I'd not looked in the second bag. So I upended it, right there on Cameron's sofa.

And it was all win.

Dildos, cock rings, prostate probes, more condoms and massage oils. There were three pairs of eyes on me and I grinned at them, holding up a black dildo and prostate wand. "I call dibs!"

Rachel and Simona laughed, but Cameron ignored me completely. I rolled my eyes at him, even though he didn't see and I packed up the bag of spilled goodies. I put it to the side, out of the way, hoping I'd get to test the products later... on a more personal level.

So instead, I started rifling through boxes, pulling out files when I noticed Cameron setting up a digital clock looking thing. He plugged it in and looked at his wrist-watch, then set the time.

Only it didn't tell the time. That much was obvious. It counted it backwards.

There were numbers, big, red and flashing. 63:47.

Fuck. 63 hours and 47 minutes until the meeting with Lurex.

"Oh, hell no," I said. "I can't work with that thing ticking down at me." Cameron stared at me, then dismissed me as though I never spoke. So I repeated, "I said, I can't work with that-"

"I heard what you said," he interrupted, as though I

bored him. "When I'm on a deadline I like to know how I'm travelling. The clock stays."

I glared at him, the smug sonnova bitch, but he didn't even look at me. I looked to Simona and Rachel, who didn't know where to look, and I huffed in defeat.

Biting my tongue, I picked up the whiteboard marker and started my usual brainstorm-progression chart, when Cameron finally looked at me and spoke. "That's not how I do that," he said.

I looked at his countdown clock. 63:45. "Well, you're going to be extremely disappointed for the next sixty-three hours and forty-five minutes."

Then he glared at me.

I smiled.

The two girls interrupted. Rachel first. "Right. Cameron you sit there," she pointed to my seat, "so Lucas has his back to the clock. You can see it, but he can't."

Simona added, "Lucas, add time increments to the bottom of your chart so Cameron can track his schedule."

He stared at me, and I stared at him. Neither of us moved.

Rachel scowled. "Christ, you two are like children. It's called compromise, and if you'd like to win the Lurex contract without killing each other in the meantime, then fucking deal with it."

Cameron glared at me. I think he might have snarled, but he picked up his papers and moved his seat in exchange for mine.

I rolled my eyes, but added his precious time incre-ments to my chart, slotting in allocated time allowances for each task.

The two girls smiled in victory, and for the next two and

a half hours, the four of us worked in silence. Surprisingly, it wasn't strained, it was productive.

We ordered Thai food, and when it arrived, with the table covered in papers, we opted to sit on the living room floor. The mood was different then. Simona asked questions about my family, my job in Dallas and how I was finding Chicago. Rachel listened and contributed occasionally, and even Cameron seemed interested.

He sat with his legs outstretched, crossed at the ankles, and the difference between the man in front of me and the one I worked with was like night and day. He laughed as we all talked, picked at everyone else's food with his chopsticks, tasting a bit of everything, and his eyes shone when he smiled.

For a moment, I thought I could even like the guy.

Grinning, Rachel said, "Care to explain the hat tipping thing, Mr. Hensley?"

I laughed. "Ah, the trademark hat tip," I said, giving her an exaggerated tip of an imaginary hat. She and Simona both smiled. "I've done it since I was a kid," I told them. "When I was little, there used to be an old man who sat outside the general store, and every time I'd walk in there with my Mom, he'd tip an invisible hat. He wouldn't say a word, just do this hat-tipping thing. My Mom would smile for a full five minutes. It made all the ladies smile." I smiled myself as I recalled. "When I was about six, I did it to Mrs. Barnett at the grocery store, and she gave me a lollipop for being a gentleman."

Rachel and Simona both laughed, and Cameron rolled his eyes. I smiled and told them seriously, "It's been getting me what I want ever since."

Simona still giggled, but asked, "You do it to make the

ladies smile? Isn't that a bit redundant? Isn't it the men you want to charm?"

I noticed Simona's eyes dart to Cameron's, whose eyes widened at Simona's words, but I grinned at her. "It's not the dipping of my hat men want. I have other ways to charm them," I said suggestively. "But I think I speak for all men, gay or straight, when I say it's never redundant to see a lady smile. Isn't that right, Cameron?"

He balked at my words at first then declared, "Um... we've got a deadline to meet."

The happy mood and free-flowing conversation died right there. Mr. All-Work-and-No-Play was becoming a very dull boy, indeed.

We started packing up the empty dinner containers, and Simona said, "Well, this is where you two do your thing." Then she indicated between herself and Rachel and said, "We've covered all the bases, done all the homework, and so we'll leave you two to it."

Rachel looked a little surprised by this, but a quick glance from Simona had her agreeing. She smiled and said, "Put those two handsome heads together and come up with an ad campaign that'll blow Lurex away."

Simona told us they'd call tomorrow to see if we needed anything and as she pulled Rachel out the door with her, I called out and stopped them. "Here, girls. Lucky pick," I said, holding up the first brown paper bag filled with Lurex goodies. Of course, they thought I was joking, so I gave the bag a shake. "Take a pick. We've got condoms; fluro, glow in the dark and if you're lucky enough, extra large," I gave them an eyebrow waggle. "Flavored lube?"

Neither of them moved. "Oh, come on," I whined. "Don't make me tell the boss of Lurex I couldn't even give their product away."

With a collective eye-roll and cheeky grin, they both grabbed a handful each, not even looking at what they took. I told them, "Take two at bed time and two before breakfast." I walked them to do the door and watched them giggle all the way to the car.

And then it was just Cameron and me.

"Are you always so forthright?" Cameron asked, seemingly not amused.

"Yes. Are you always so... guarded?"

Cameron was quiet for a long moment, and I was beginning to regret the question. Then he answered.

"Yes."

CHAPTER THREE

I AM... SPEECHLESS

61:03

Cameron started cataloguing products and target markets with existing campaigns against Lurex's financial reports, while I started some background research on Lurex and on our competition. And, more importantly, background research on those we would be meeting with on Monday morning.

59:28

The head of marketing for Lurex was a guy by the name of Charles Makenna. I tracked him, where he had been and what he had done over the last few years. If he was the guy who'd be hiring us, I needed to know as much as I could about him; what he wore, what car he drove, what he ate for breakfast.

Cameron researched color schemes for product design, taking into account market research with Fletcher Advertising's art division, art exhibits and even fashion catwalks. If there was a color trend buyers were leaning toward, he'd find it.

And we were making good time.

58:47

I grabbed two beers, handed one to Cameron, kicked my boots off and took my laptop to sit on the floor leaning against the sofa. After a few more minutes of my scouting web pages, I found a very interesting pattern just as Cameron grumbled about me surfing the net and not doing a goddamn constructive thing.

"Bingo!" I cried.

"What?"

"I just found our target market."

"And?"

"Mr. Charles Makenna, the head of Lurex Marketing – the guy we were both meeting on Monday – has been wracking up the frequent flyer points. Every year, for the last four years, he's been in Sydney, Australia in February, Chicago and London in June, and Montreal, Canada in August."

"So?"

"Is it a fluke he takes annual leave and international vacations that coincide with Mardi Gras and National Pride?" I smiled victoriously. "I think not. And look at these pictures," I pointed to each one, "a gold band on his ring finger, but the recurring woman does not. I'd bet anything you like she's his PA, or his cover story if you will. Because Mr. Makenna is gay."

Cameron blinked. Three times.

Then he looked at me. His cool, stoic face gave nothing away. It was his game face. "And you think we should push the gay market?"

"Absolutely."

Cameron swallowed thickly and sat down on the floor across from me, his feet at my thigh... his long, long, size at-least-eleven feet... I shook my head and forced my eyes from his feet to his face. I could almost hear the cogs turning in his head. He looked anything but convinced.

I pushed the idea. "A twin campaign. Keeping the hetero line, but adding a gay line with matching concepts. Whatever we have a het couple doing, we have a gay couple doing the exact same thing. If we can show Makenna we believe there's no difference between the two couples, we've won his respect before we even open our mouths."

Cameron tilted his head and then did the oddest thing. He smiled. "Not bad."

"It's brilliant, and you know it."

He rolled his eyes. "Not unsure of yourself, are you?"

"What's to be unsure of?" I questioned sarcastically, rolling my eyes back at him. "I mean, when I first started at Fletcher Advertising, it was a shock for me not to be the best, or the most confident, most conceited man there." I looked pointedly at him.

His eyes widened. "Me?"

I nodded. Then he said, "Best, confident *and* conceited. Gee, is that a compliment or an insult?"

"Both," I said and gave him a smirk. "It wasn't hard to be jealous of Cameron Fletcher."

"Jealous?" his eyes popped, and he looked genuinely surprised. Which was odd, because at work he was the King of cool, calm and collected. But outside of work, from what I'd seen, he was the polar opposite.

"In case you haven't noticed, which I suspect you have, is that the men who meet you want to *be* you, and the women who meet you, want to *be with* you."

Cameron shook his head, dismissing me. He scoffed, "And you don't have it good?"

Now it was my eyes that widened. "Me?"

He snorted. "You are who you are. No apologies. That

takes fucking guts. And my father seems to think you're something special."

Ah, and now the truth. "Is that why you don't like me?"

His eyes popped. "What?"

"When we first met," I told him, trying to act casual, taking a swig of my beer. "After I'd met with you and your father, you glared at me like I'd done something to personally offend you."

His face twisted. "I didn't hate you," he said quietly. He cleared his throat. "I was... jealous."

Jealous?

"Huh?"

He smiled a sad smile. "You walked into that meeting, looked my father straight in the eye and said, 'I'm gay, like it or lump it' like it was the easiest thing in the world."

"So?"

He was quiet for a while, then he shrugged. "Never mind."

"Just fucking say it, Cameron."

He swallowed, and for a second I thought he wasn't going to. But he did. "I've wanted to say those very words to him for years."

I'm gay, like it or lump it.

I'm gay... like it... or lump it....

Holy.

Shit.

"Are you...?"

His eyes were glued to his fidgeting hands, but he nodded.

Holy. Shit.

And everything became crystal fucking clear; why he didn't like me. Wait, scratch that. He didn't *not* like me. He was envious. Of me. Holy shit. The glances between him and Simona? There was no history between them. She knew.

"Simona knows," I said quietly.

He nodded. "No one else."

"Your parents? Your dad?"

He gave a tight shake of his head, misery clear on his face. "No."

"Holy shit," was about all I could say.

"And now *you* know," he whispered. "I'd appreciate it if you-"

"I won't tell anyone," I promised him. "Scouts honour," I declared, holding up two fingers to my forehead.

"It's three fingers," he mumbled.

I shrugged, and he smiled. I wasn't sure what to say... "So," I hedged, "seeing anyone?"

He snorted. "No. Not for a while. No one serious anyway. There was a guy for a while... about a year actually," he said quietly. "His name was Liam. But he wanted me to come out and he was sick of hiding. Couldn't say I blame him. But I... I just couldn't."

We sat in silence for a while, as his admission sunk into my brain.

Fuck.

"Why me? Why tell me?" I asked. "It's not like we're..." I tried to think of the right word. "It's not like we're close or anything."

He was still looking at his hands, but I could see his eyebrows meet as he frowned. His voice was soft, and I almost didn't hear him. "I thought you'd understand."

His words stunned me. I couldn't think of a single fucking thing to say. Well, nothing intelligent or profound anyway.

"Gay?"

He smiled, vulnerable, and he shrugged one shoulder. "Yeah."

"I so had you pegged as straight."

"I'm pretty good at acting the part," he admitted quietly. "That's me, selling the unsellable."

Unsellable?

He took a deep breath and said, "Simona's been onto me for months... to speak to you. But I didn't have a clue what to say, how to broach the subject, or how you'd react. For all I knew, you could have laughed at me. Which thankfully, you haven't yet."

I was, for the first time in my life, speechless. This fucking God of a man was sitting in front of me, baring his very soul, and I was at a loss for words.

So, unsure of what else to fucking do, I picked up his foot and pulled it into my lap. He was startled by my actions, but I looked him square in the eye as I pulled his shoe off and started massaging his socked foot. He looked at me, somewhat bewildered, but as I dug my thumbs into the sole of his foot, rubbing circles into his perfect arches, his eyes soon closed and he hummed.

"Cameron, I would never laugh at you. Never," I told him seriously. "Not about something like that."

But then I looked at his foot.

And I laughed.

Cameron's eyes opened, and he stared at me, offended, I think. But I was looking at his foot, well, at his sock.

"What the fuck is on your sock?"

"Oh," he sighed with a relieved chuckle. "Um, it's Charlie Brown."

Charlie Brown? He wears two thousand dollar suits and *cartoon socks?* "Do I even want to know who's on the other foot?"

He smiled and lifted his other foot, offering it to me.

I pulled his shoe off. "Linus?"

He smiled and said, "I had to buy two different pairs so I'd have a set with Charlie and Linus."

I shook my head at him, but started to massage that foot too. He grinned and closed his eyes as I pressed my thumbs into the ball of his foot. "You have talented thumbs," he said with a quiet moan.

"You're not the first person to tell me that," I told him, and his eyebrow lifted, though his eyes didn't open.

I watched him as he simply allowed himself to feel, with his eyes closed, his head lolled back and a slight curl to his lips, he sure was something to look at. If someone told me that morning I'd be sitting on the floor in Cameron Fletcher's house, massaging his feet, I'd have thought they'd lost their fucking mind.

He opened his eyes and looked at me. "So," he said casually. "You know my secret. Tell me something about Lucas Hensley that no one knows."

Uh oh.

Well, shit.

Fair's fair, I guessed. I took a deep breath. "I um... I have... a thing for feet?" My uncertainty made it sound like a question. His eyes popped open, darting from my face to his feet; one in my hands, the other resting in my lap.

"*Feet?* Really?" he said with a smile. I glared at him. He grinned, but his eyes were warm, kind.

"I can stop massaging if that's a problem..." I trailed off, teasing.

He wiggled his toes and laughed. "No problem. Not a one."

He stretched the foot in my hand, flexing it and wiggled

his toes. Then he did the same to the foot on my thigh. I couldn't be totally sure, but I think he was playing.

So I held his foot with both hands and start rubbing it in a pumping motion. It took a moment for him to realize, but I could see it in his eyes when he did. They widened, then darkened and fuck me, I think we had ourselves a moment.

All too soon, he pulled both feet away and cleared his throat. "Uh, it's late," he said quickly, looking at the clock.

I checked my watch. It was almost two AM. I wasn't sure if being sequestered with him included staying overnight. I yawned and asked, "What time do you want me back here in the morning?"

He blinked, stood up and walked quickly to the table. "Um, you're welcome to stay here. It makes better sense." He tidied up piles of paperwork, and he was back to being all business. "We'll need to start early. I'll be setting my alarm for six."

He didn't say as much, but I presumed I was to do the same.

"You can have the guest room," he said, walking toward the door near the stairs.

I wasn't really sure if I should stay or leave, but the next fifty-seven hours and twenty-six minutes would be intense enough without adding bad manners to the mix. "If you're sure," I said with a smile. "That'd be great. I did pack an overnight bag. It's in my car."

I raced out to my car to get it, and he waited for me at the door. As I walked inside, he flicked the light switch leaving downstairs in darkness, so I couldn't be sure, but I think he smiled before turning into the hall. Upstairs, he showed me the bathroom, and then the guest room, and he was acting a little weird. I was adept at reading people, and

I think I was witnessing something rarely seen... Cameron Fletcher, nervous.

He walked toward what I presumed was his bedroom door, and I called out, "Cameron?" He turned, and I told him, "I just wanted to say thank you."

Without a word, he raised an eyebrow in question.

I told him sincerely, "For being honest with me, for telling me you're gay. It took guts." Then I asked him, "You must feel relieved someone else knows?"

He looked at me, honest and vulnerable, but he smiled and nodded. Without another word, he disappeared into his room.

I stripped down to my underwear and climbed into bed. I lay there, thinking about the anomaly that was Cameron Fletcher. He was fucking gay! How did I not notice *that?* I considered for a moment my gay-dar might be broken – it had been a while, give me a fucking break. But I soon realized, I never really noticed *him* at all. Not really. All I saw was the man he wanted people to see; the suit, the women who surrounded him, women who tripped over themselves to be near him, the accounts he secured, the deals he made.

I wondered idly if the competitiveness between us would lessen any, now that we'd bonded a little. Maybe now he'd see me as more of an ally, rather than someone he has to try and compete with.

But I set my alarm to wake up ten minutes before him, just in case.

CHAPTER FOUR

I AM... JUST GETTING STARTED

52:00

It was barely six in the morning when I woke to the realization that I was not in my bed. Then I remembered... Cameron. I could hear the shower, so he'd either set his alarm to wake before me, or he didn't sleep much.

I never woke up in a particularly good mood. But figuring I may as well get started, I headed downstairs in search of caffeine and started looking through kitchen cupboards to see if I could find coffee. I sniffed out ground beans, cups and the machine, and set it to warm.

Whether it was curiosity, or a need to know more behind the man, even though I said I wasn't going to, I checked out the photos on display in Cameron's living room. I presumed they were mostly family photos, some friends maybe, but definitely no Cameron-as-a-couple snaps.

He was gay. Jesus. Of all the things I'd have expected to come out of his mouth, that wasn't one of them.

I had no idea. Literally, none.

Even in the light of day, on about four hours sleep, it

still did my head in. I'd seen this guy every day at work, and not once did I ever suspect he was anything but straight. The way he laughed and smiled with women, how they flirted with him. And this entire time, he'd been living a lie.

I most certainly didn't envy him that.

He had been doing what he did best. Selling an image.

I felt something different toward him now. Something I didn't feel for him yesterday when I went to work. And fuck me... I think it might be respect.

By the time Cameron came downstairs, I handed him a hot cup of coffee. He was freshly showered, smelled and looked delicious, his hair its trademark artful mess. He looked at me, surprised by the gesture of coffee.

"Thank you," he said quietly, leaning against the dining table, next to me.

I gave him a smile, and then I spied his feet. Oh, fuck me. I look from his socked feet to his face. "Really? Batman and Robin? *Really*, Cameron?"

He grinned. "Really."

Holy sock fetish. I chuckled at my funny thought. "Do I even want to know what other pairings you've got?" I asked. He chuckled quietly, but I put my hand up. "No, wait. I think I should ask *why* before *what*," I said, looking at him expectantly.

"Well," he said, sipping his coffee thoughtfully. "It's the only thing that's really me under the expensive suits and straight facade."

"Gay socks?"

He laughed. "The socks aren't gay."

I begged to differ. "Well, they're not fucking straight."

"You'll think I'm crazy," he said, as he shook his head, smiling. "But everyone at work sees the *straight Cameron Fletcher*," he said. "But underneath what they see, underneath the suits and serious business, I know I'm wearing them... I'm not explaining this very well," he chuckled. Then he sighed and started again, "I wear them every day to stay true to myself."

This surprised me. I wasn't expecting there to be such a meaningful reason behind his silly socks. I nodded and smiled at him. "Good enough reason."

He shrugged and sipped his coffee.

With my cup in hand, I walked back to the mantel with the photo frames. "Who's the couple?"

"My brother and his wife."

"How old is the photo?"

"About six months," he answered. "Why?"

"Would they do a photo shoot?"

"For?"

"Condoms."

Cameron choked on his coffee.

I gather that was a no.

I tried again anyway, "We need a straight couple for proofs. Today, Cameron."

He looked at me, then to the photo and back to me. His mouth opened and closed, twice.

I smiled. "Body shots only, no facials. They'll be unrecognizable."

His shoulders slumped. "Do you have any idea how difficult he will make my life for the next twelve months?"

I put my coffee down. "More difficult than your dad if we don't score this contract?"

It was a low blow, and we both knew it. He scowled at me, but I had won. He knew it, because he sighed in defeat.

"If they're the straight couple, who will we use as the gay couple?" he asked flatly.

I grinned hugely at him and waggled my eyebrows suggestively.

Now, he was an intelligent man, it didn't take him long to figure it out. The coffee cup stopped half way to his open mouth, and he stared at me, unblinking, unmoving – except for the twitch in the corner of his eye.

Trying not to laugh, I said, "I'll just have a quick shower while you call your brother." When I got to the door, I turned and asked, "Have you got a camera? We're gonna need..."

I didn't bother finishing my sentence. He still hadn't moved. Or blinked. He should probably put the coffee down before he dropped it.

And he really should see someone about that twitch in his eye.

48:00

Cameron sighed into his phone. "Simona, I have to go. They're here. Wish me luck." I have no idea what Simona said to him, but his eyes darted to mine, and he sighed again before saying goodbye to her. She was a good assistant, I'd give her that. Like my Rachel; organized, smart and seemed to know what I wanted done before I asked her for it. I'd not long spoken to her, promising we were being good boys, playing fair and being well-behaved. Saying goodbye, I told her I'd call her if I needed anything.

Cameron opened the front door, and his unsuspecting brother and sister-in-law walked inside, stopping when they saw me. Cameron made introductions, "Ben, Ashley, this is Lucas."

I smiled and said hello with a tip of my imaginary hat. Ben looked at Cameron, a little confused, but Ashley looked at me and smiled, knowingly it would seem. Oh, hell no. She thought I was here with Cameron, as in with *with* him.

Which meant Simona wasn't the only one who knew where Cameron's preferences lay.

"Lucas Hensley. I work with Cameron," I explained for everyone's benefit. "We're working now actually, which is why Cameron phoned. It was my idea."

They both looked at me. I figured that if Cameron was putting the relationship with his brother on the line, I may as well take the blame. "We're desperate for a couple to be in a photo shoot for a product campaign."

Cameron chimed in, "Dad's lined up a one-off meeting for an exclusive contract and gave us sixty-five hours to run an entire campaign."

Ben shrugged. Ashley clued in first. "What's the product?"

I looked her straight in the eye. "Condoms and lubrication."

Their reactions were fucking comical to watch. Even Cameron nearly smiled at their reaction. Until Ben spun around and glared at his brother. "What the fuck?"

But I kept talking. "Lurex is offering an advertising contract, and your father wants it. We're pushing to get this done and would really value your input."

Ben stared at me and then back at Cameron. "Is he serious?"

Cameron nodded, but I could see this wasn't going to be easy. I realized my best sell was Ashley. If she was on board, Ben would do it. I looked at her, "Still shots, torso only, no breasts, no facial shots. You both will have the final say as to the pictures chosen. I promise no one outside of this room will know who it is. Full discretion. It will be tasteful, you have my word."

"What's in it for us?" she asked.

"Ashley?" Ben cried, staring at her with wide eyes.

But I answered her with, "A warm fuzzy feeling inside from helping Cameron, and two box-seat season tickets to the Bears."

I was given the tickets as part of a deal last month... I never really liked football anyway.

47:30

"I can't believe I'm doing this," Ben grumbled.

"I can't believe you're doing this in my bedroom," Cameron grumbled.

"Ashley, put your right hand higher," I instructed, looking through the viewfinder.

They were on Cameron's bed, on their knees, both shirtless. Ben was well-built, solid and took obvious care in his body. Ashley was petite. They couldn't have been more perfect.

Ben had his back to me, and all I could see of Ashley was her arm, the side of her hip and her long blond hair. Fucking textbook-perfect.

I took some side on shots. Ben's arm or Ashley's hair hid bra straps, giving the impression of nudity. There were shots of Ben's front, with Ashley's fingertips slipping under the waistband of his jeans, Ben's huge hands on his wife's tiny waist and a rear view of Ashley, her head thrown back, with Ben's arms wrapped around her.

I even managed to score some shots of their feet. And it gave me an idea.

"Okay, Ben," I called out. "You can put your shirt back on."

I handed Ashley her shirt, but asked her to keep her jeans off. "I need your feet, please."

I had them stand, embracing. Ben's masculine feet lined by the hem of his jeans while Ashley had one foot between

Ben's, the other foot resting on top of his. Her painted toenails were perfectly feminine by contrast.

Then I took shots of them lying down, with Ashley's dainty feet entangled with Ben's.

Cameron stood at the door, seemingly uncomfortable with the whole idea.

Ben griped, "What the fuck did we have to strip down to our underwear for if you just wanted photos of our feet?"

"Oh," I said with a smile. "Because you have beautiful feet."

Ben looked at Ashley and nudged her. "Hear that, honey? You have beautiful feet."

Changing the settings on Cameron's camera, I looked up at him and chuckled. "Oh yes, Ashley does too."

It took a long second, but Ben gaped, Ashley giggled, and I looked to the door to see Cameron's reaction, but he was already walking down the stairs.

46:20

Cameron and Ben were in the kitchen ordering lunch. Cameron was paying, so Ben's list was long.

Ashley and I were sitting at the dining table. "You're very good," Ashley said, as we scrolled through the digital pictures. "I like this one... and that one..." she was selecting her preference of photos we could use. She had a good eye for detail, and I liked the ones she chose. "The feet shots are great," she said. "They really show a couple being intimate without the details."

I smiled. "That is exactly what I want it to show."

"Very clever," she said with a smile.

I explained, "I've been to enough photo shoots and seen enough ad campaigns to know what works, but I'm no photographer. I'll have to digi-shop these before we do anything."

Past caring, Ben left the decision to his wife, and Ashley approved fifteen shots in all. I slid a disc into my laptop as I explained in detail, what I'd be doing with the photos for the next eight or so hours. When the disc was finished burning, I handed it to her. "Here," I said. "A copy of all the photos. Do with them what you will." I winked at her, and she giggled.

"So, you and Cameron spend a bit of time together...?" she asked quietly, suggestively.

Ooh, yep. She knew.

"Only at work," I said. "And even then, not much. This campaign," I said, indicating to the files on the table next to us, "is the only thing we've ever talked about."

"But you are gay, right?" she asked quietly, with a smile.

"That I am, Ma'am."

She nodded. "I guessed as much."

Smirking, I raised my eyebrow in question, and she explained, "I was just semi-naked, upstairs in a room with you, and I can assure you, it wasn't me you were checking out."

I chuckled and nodded. "True. Your husband's a good looking guy."

"So is my brother-in-law," she said smugly. "Don't you think?"

I rolled my eyes. "He's not *good-looking*," I amended. "He's beautiful."

She smiled sadly. "I wish he'd get out more. He needs someone, ya know? He's been alone for too long. All he does is work."

"Well, our jobs don't exactly leave a lot of time for a social life." I looked at that Goddamn countdown clock. "We'll both be working for the next 46 hours to get this done."

Then she looked around to make sure Cameron and Ben were still both out of earshot. She whispered, "Can't you take him out? Take him to a bar, get him drunk, find him some tall, dark and handsome stranger..." then she looked me up and down and amends, "or some tall, Southern blond...?"

I laughed. But I had to admit, it was a fucking good idea.

CHAPTER FIVE

I AM... NOT DRUNK ENOUGH.

39:20 (8:40 PM Saturday night)

"Cameron," I said, *again*, as I rummaged through his wardrobe. "We are doing this."

His lips pursed into a thin line, and he huffed. He wanted to go, I could tell. But he was fucking scared. Not that he'd admit to that.

I changed my approach. "It's strictly for work. Think of it as product marketing; focus group, target research. We don't have to stay long."

I could see his want warring with reservation in his eyes, but he wouldn't give in. Jesus, he was a hard sell.

I pulled out a shirt and sighed. "All right Cameron," I said, all out of patience. "Feel free to stay here. But I have had my head in this fucking account for over twenty-four hours straight. I'm going cross-eyed looking at that damn computer screen doing those photos. I am going out," I said, leaving no room for argument. "There's at least two or three gay clubs, and hopefully, several men that are about to be Hensleyed."

I pulled my tee-shirt over my head and threw it onto

Cameron's bed. I held his shirt up, pretending to give it a once over, but really giving him plenty of time to get an eyeful of me shirtless. I waited until his eyes went from my chest to my face before I smiled. He looked away quickly, like he didn't like what he saw, but a faint blush gave him away. Grinning, I pulled on the shirt I had in my hand. It was one of Cameron's.

He cleared his throat. "That's a gym shirt," Cameron informs me.

Oh, please. It was a tight-fitting, black, sleeveless shirt that showed my pecs and biceps perfectly and probably cost more than most people earn in a day. I grinned at him, "With a bit of luck, I won't have it on for long."

He swallowed and blinked, and I knew I almost had him.

I walked past him, headed back downstairs, pulled on my boots and picked up the first bag of Lurex goodies. I gave Cameron a wink. "For research purposes only, of course."

His jaw bulged as he clenched his teeth, and his nostrils flared. I think it was his pissed off look, but whatever it was, it was fucking hot. He growled, "I'll go if we're home by twelve."

"Two," I countered.

"One."

"Fine."

He sneered at me, but he took the stairs two at a time and came back down half a minute later. He was wearing his blue jeans and dark grey tee-shirt. It was nothing extraordinary, but seeing him dressed in something other than a button down shirt was something kinda special.

Especially one that hugged him just right.

I obviously got caught staring.

"What?" he said defensively. "I do work out."

"I can tell," I said, drawing my eyes from his head to his feet. Well, to his socks... his multi-colored striped Sesame Street socks....

"Bert and Ernie? *Really?* For the love of God and Armani, I need to buy you some socks."

He grinned spectacularly. "Don't knock the socks." Then he pulled his loafers on and stood. "We're leaving by one AM, this is for research purposes only, and *no* drinking."

37:15

"Two scotches, straight, please," I ordered over the bar, and handed one straight to Cameron.

He rolled his eyes, but took it. It was his third, and I think he was a little drunk. He had been like a kid in a candy store since we walked in, eyeing every type of *candy* he possibly could. And they were eyeing him too... well, more like eye fucking him.

Couldn't say I blamed them. He was a fucking stand out. His sculpted face, his just-fucked hair, he didn't even have to try. He was just fucking beautiful.

He'd been so nervous when we arrived. He'd almost hid behind me, like he was going to be seen by someone who recognized him. "Come on, Cameron," I'd said softly. "You have the perfect excuse to finally go clubbing, drink a little, dance a little... this is completely work-related. We're here strictly on business."

He'd rolled his eyes and exhaled loudly, but at least I got him to walk through the door.

I'd shown the security guy what I had in the paper grocery bag. The big, burly guy looked at the bag of condoms, then at us. "Little ambitious, yeah?"

I gave him a wink and a tip of my imaginary hat. "I *never* get my ambitions mixed up with my capabilities."

He smiled, shook his head at me and waved us through. That was about an hour ago.

Cameron had had a few drinks. I could tell he wanted to dance, but he didn't have the nerve to just walk out onto the dance floor into a sea of all those men by himself. The place wasn't even too busy yet. I needed to wait just a little longer....

So I decided to ask Cameron some questions. It wasn't entirely unfortunate I had to lean in real close so he could hear. "Did you ever go out clubbing with... whatshisname?" I remembered the guy's name, Liam, but acting like his ex was forgettable seemed like a good idea.

Cameron frowned and shook his head. "No... he wanted to..."

Jesus. "Did you go out *at all*? Dinner or movies?"

He swallowed down his scotch, draining it. I could smell it lingering on his breath.

"No. Unless we went away, out of town," he said.

Jesus H Christ.

"Is it any wonder he dumped me?" he said loudly in my ear, speaking over the music.

I was hoping that was a rhetorical question, because I sure as hell didn't want to answer it. Instead, I said, "But spending all that time indoors had its benefits too, right?"

He huffed at me, but he gave me half a smile. "Yeah, I guess it did."

I laughed. "I'm sure it did. So," I said, looking around the crowd, "see anyone you might want to spend some time indoors with?"

His brow pinched again, and he almost frowned. "I thought we were here to work," he said. And he realized at the same time I did, just how close we were standing -

almost touching... almost. And he took a step back, away from me, putting some distance between us.

The club was starting to fill with bodies, some fully dressed, some not. I pretended to scout the floor, but I was really just watching Cameron, when some random guy approached him and asked him to dance. He wasn't bad looking, in a Where's Waldo kind of way. And I was torn. Did I intervene? Did I tell this will-never-be-worthy guy to fuck off, or did I let Cameron go with him?

Before I could comment, Cameron said the darnedest thing. "I'm kinda here with someone."

I'm kinda here with someone.

Me.

He was kinda here with me.

I didn't even try to stop the grin. 'Where's Waldo' disappeared in the crowd, which was three scotches worth of funny, and I laughed.

"What?" he snapped.

I cocked my head to the side and looked at him. "If you're here with me, then you'll dance with me."

"N-n-n-o, I can't," he said, shaking his head.

"Bullshit," I called him on it. Stepping right up close to him, his face was barely an inch from mine, I said, "There's nothing you can't do."

And we had ourselves another one of those moments. Right there. He stared at me, seriously, but in a with-promise kind of way, and I stared right back at him.

He swallowed and looked away, breaking our stare. "Maybe another drink...?"

I smiled. "Sure."

This time when he handed me my drink, I took it with my right hand and rested my left on the small of his back.

Leaning in, right up close, I spoke into his ear. "Work first. Then we dance."

"What do you have in mind?" he asked. I could feel the warmth of his breath on the skin of my neck.

"Close, slow dancing, grinding hips, wandering hands."

I could feel him freeze. After two heartbeats he said, "I meant with work. What did you have in mind with work?"

I pulled back a little, so I could see his face, and I smiled. "Oh, that..."

He looked away, but the corners of his lips curled as he tried not to smile.

I finished my drink in one mouthful and waited for Cameron to do the same before I took his hand, pulling him through the crowd toward the stage to the DJ's box.

I jumped up on the stage, but Cameron didn't do the same. I turned and looked at him, and he stared at me, somewhat bewildered. "What the *hell* do you think you're doing?"

I grinned and winked at him, then leaned over and beckoned the DJ. I laid on the Southern charm, winked and punctuated each compliment with dimples. I also asked for five minutes of floor time. I handed him a handful of Lurex goodies, threw in a cock ring and he killed the music.

Just like that.

Every man on the dance floor and those at the bar, turned and faced us. This was it.

Now or never.

"Good evening, boys," I started. "Would y'all help out a Southern boy tonight? I need a little assistance."

There were a few calls about exactly how some would like to *help* me, in a physically gratifying way. It made me smile and chuckle shyly, all for show of course.

"First," I said loudly, "I need my partner in crime up here with me." I pointed to Cameron, who looked a cross between mortified and livid. I walked over, extended my hand to him and said, "Would the sexiest man in the room please get his sexy ass up here?"

He took my hand, mumbled something about, "the fuck I'm doing," but climbed on the stage to stand beside me. And cue more applause and wolf whistles.

Cameron whisper-shouted in my ear, "You fucking owe me."

"Just start recording," I hissed to him.

And he did. He pulled his phone out of his pocket, thumbed the screen to the camera settings, and he started to film.

I turned back to the crowd. "Okay boys, I have some real quick questions." I reached into the bag of condoms and lube, pulled out a random sample, and held it up for them all to see. "Standard Lurex products... you've all seen them. You've all used them. I want to know what you *don't* like about them."

Silence. Fucking silence.

Shit.

They needed some hedging. "You want to know what *I* hate about the standard product packaging?"

This time it was a focused silence. They were listening at least.

"I hate that every Goddamn couple on a pack of rubbers is straight."

Silence. Again.

Then someone broke. "Hell yeah!" some guy yelled. So I handed him a condom. Then the others started calling out things out, and each time I passed out a handful of foil packets of condoms and lube samples.

"Yeah, I don't want no pictures of women in my bedroom."

"Yeah, where's the pictures of two guys?"

"Why don't companies use pictures of two men on their rubbers?

"Because no franger company has the balls to do it, that's why!"

Perfect. But I needed to control the direction of this survey. "How much money per week would you spend on these products?"

"Ten bucks."

"Fifteen."

"Twenty."

"Fifty!"

"Liar."

"I'm an over achiever!" the guy defended himself.

"Here!" I called out to him, holding up a variety of foil packets. "In the name of financial assistance and safe sex, please take a handful."

And so the impromptu Q&A went, all on film. I asked them questions until there were no condoms or lube left. Not in that bag, anyway.

We'd read these statistics a hundred times, seen them in black and white in all the Lurex files we'd memorized in the last twenty-four hours.

But to hear it from the source was raw, unedited and a little bit brilliant.

I thanked the crowd for their time and patience, gave them all a tip of my imaginary hat and ask Mr. Maestro to please make the pretty boys dance.

It was then I looked at Cameron. He was smiling, and staring straight at me. Even over the start of the beat, beat, beat of the music, I could hear what he said. "That was..."

"Fucking brilliant?" I prompted.

He grinned and shook his head. "I was going to say it was a pleasure to watch."

Holy shit. I think Cameron Fletcher just gave me a compliment. Either that, or he just flirted with me. Well, whichever it was, it made me smile.

The double dimpled kind of smile.

There really was so much I could have said or implied, but I settled for leaning right up close to his ear. I told him, "First we drink." I pulled back so I could look into his eyes. Our faces were close, his eyes were dark.

I smiled. "Then we dance."

CHAPTER SIX

I AM...AMBIDEXTROUS

40 : ... something hours... I had no fucking idea what the time was. Five scotches and a drunk Cameron had me not caring a great deal.

"Why don't we just film other guys?" Cameron asked loudly in my ear, talking over the music. He was nervous, trying to get out of dancing with me. But he couldn't fool me.

He fucking wanted to. He wasn't protesting *that* much.

It was there, in his eyes; bright, and keen, swimming amidst five shots of scotch. I leaned in to talk in his ear. "Because I don't have a legal disclaimer handy. I don't want them to sue us next week, and we're *not* paying them." I stood back, grinning at him, and I spoke loud enough so he could hear me. "And I'm out of free condoms!"

When the barman gave me round number six, I ordered one more. I turned around to give Cameron his drink, which I clinked with my glass, and I knocked mine back in one mouthful. I put my empty glass back on the bar, and Cameron was watching me, my face, my hands. He was seriously checking me out, and that made me happier than it should.

Grinning, I shrugged at him. "Now, drink up! We've got work to do."

He downed the liquor, squinting at the burn, and when his eyes reopened, they were slow and languid. I wasn't much of a drinker, and from what I could tell, Cameron was even less so. I had a heady buzz, the room was a pretty mass of color, sound and men.

But I think Cameron was a little more than tipsy.

He had a lazy smirk and a faraway look in his eyes. And I think he just went from beautiful to cute.

Could he be both?

He giggled, and that was a definite fucking 'yes'. He was most definitely beautiful *and* cute.

"You alright there?" I asked him, unable to help but smile at him. He smiled back at me and nodded. "What's so funny?"

He chuckled again and shook his head. "I can't believe I'm here," he said. "With you."

With me. That was an odd thing to add. "Something wrong with being here? *With me?*"

He shook his head. "Absolutely not," he said. "Never thought in a hundred years I would be, that's all."

I had kinda forgot this was rare for him, being in a gay clubs full of half naked men. "Then we shall have to come back," I said. "After this Lurex deal is done, you and I will go out again."

He swallowed and nodded, and then he smiled. I couldn't tell whether it was an unsure I-don't-think-so smile, or a shy I-think-I'd-like-that smile. And I couldn't, for the life of me, figure out which one I wanted it to be. Did I want to socialize with a guy, who up until this time yesterday, I didn't even like? Did I want us to go back to how we were? Not talking, sneering at each other, or did I want to get to know this guy?

I was pretty fucking sure I knew it was the latter. And when I said *get to know this guy*, I meant get to know him very, *very* well....

"Here," I added, handing him his other drink, before my over-thinking brain got away from me. I picked up my drink, and before Cameron had a sip of his, I'd finished mine. Yeah, so I'd pay for it tomorrow, but I'd deal with that then. Tomorrow.

I needed to get through tonight first.

I looked at the guys around us, scouting for someone who looked trustworthy enough. And I found him... or, rather, her. I called her over, and she shimmied over to where we were standing.

"Hi gorgeous girl," I laid on the Texan accent. "Would you mind helping out a Southern boy in distress?"

"Oh, sugar," she said dramatically, putting her hand over her heart. "What *can* a girl do to help?"

I looked at Cameron and wished I could take a photo. It was fucking priceless. He was staring at the drag-queen, almost gaping. He blinked, then he blinked again.

"Lucas and Cameron," I said, making introductions.

To which she replied, flamboyantly, "Ellie Tzar." Her cocoa-colored skin was highlighted by her pink bouffant hairdo and matching eye shadow, lipstick and sequin dress. She was fantastic.

"Well, Ellie Tzar," I continued, pulling Cameron closer. "My boy here and I need someone to film us dance."

That grabbed Cameron's attention. He stopped gaping at the woman beside us and was now gaping at me.

I looked back at Ellie and told her, "See, we're trying to

get some Pride out there in the commercial world of advertising. We think it's about time the real world saw the real us," I said, waving my hand to the club of men. "Just some raw footage on this here phone, right here on the dance floor. Fifteen minutes of your time?"

Ellie nodded enthusiastically, giving a short spiel on how it was about sweet time someone took a stand against corporate giants and how brave we were to try.

I didn't bother telling her there was a fine line between brave and crazy, and come 10:15 Monday morning, I wasn't sure on which side of the line we'd be standing.

I gave her a tip of my imaginary hat. "Darlin', we'd be most grateful."

She smiled all shy like, batted her fake eyelashes and said, "Well now, who can turn down a gentleman such as you?"

See, selling ice to Eskimos. Really, it was what I was born to do.

I took off my shirt and tucked it into my back pocket.

Aaaand, Cameron was back to gaping. At me, at my chest, my stomach. I looked down as I rubbed my hand over my abs, then looked directly at Cameron. "Like what you see?"

He didn't answer with words, but I could see him swallow. And that was answer enough.

"Want to know what it feels like?"

Cameron looked at me, then back to the dance floor. "Come on," I smiled at him. "I want to see Bert and Ernie in action."

He looked around, then at me, clearly confused. "Who?"

Smiling, I explained, "Your socks."

Recognition flickered in his eyes, and he chuckled,

relieved, I think. He really should relax and laugh more, because he really was fucking beautiful.

There were tiny little laugh lines at the corner of his eyes and at the edge of his pink, pink lips when he smiled. One thing six shots of scotch told me was, Cameron Fletcher redefined good looking.

Michelangelo couldn't have dreamed that shit up.

I figured this was my one and only shot at touching this real-life Statue of David. I asked Ellie to follow, and I grabbed Cameron's hand. Leading us out into the crowded dance floor, I didn't even look to see if he objected. I knew he wouldn't.

He wanted this. I fucking knew he did.

When we'd ventured far enough into the swaying mass of bodies, I turned on my heel so Cameron basically ran into me. I grabbed his waist and held him against me. His mouth fell open, but I held his gaze, waiting for him to tell me no.

Of course he fucking didn't.

I grinned at him and skimmed my hand across his stomach, trailing my fingers down to his hip. When I slid my fingers into his hip jeans pocket, his eyes popped. "What are you doing?"

He stopped, relieved, disappointed, when I pull out his phone. Sure, I could have used mine, but then I wouldn't have had the excuse to stick my hand in Cameron's pocket.

"Tempting Cameron, but we need this," I said, holding up his phone. I found the camera setting and handed it to Ellie. She was close enough so whatever footage she did get would show the crowded dance floor behind us. I wanted it unrehearsed, unchoreographed.

I looked at Ellie and using my hands, I indicated no head-shots, just torso's and hips. She nodded in understanding and called, "Action, boys."

So this was it.

Not taking my eyes off his, I slowly edged one foot between his. My hands gripped his hips, and I pressed our bodies together. His eyes were wide, and I was waiting for a flicker of hesitation or regret to tell me to stop. But there was none.

His nostrils flared, and his breath stuttered. And with no words at all, he told me to keep going.

So I started to move.

Slowly, I rocked against him to the beat of the music. I had hold of him, moving us. I was aware of Ellie filming, moving around us, but I was focused on the man in my arms. I could feel the moment he surrendered; he relaxed, moved more fluidly and his hands gripped onto my sides. I kept my face at his neck and ear, breathing into the hair at the nape of his neck.

I could feel him. All of him. His chest, his abs, his denim covered dick, his thighs, his hands on me.

I ain't gonna lie. It felt fucking good.

It felt... fucking great.

I knew he could feel my hardening cock. It should have shocked me, or at least reminded me, that I worked with this man. I had to face him in the sober light of day. But it didn't.

I wanted him to feel me.

I wanted him to know I liked it.

I wanted him to know what he was doing to me.

Then he moved his hands. One slid down my waist to grip my hip. Just when I thought he was about to stop me, his other hand slid around to the small of my back, and he pushed me closer to him.

I think I moaned.

I know I shuddered.

I know because he chuckled at my reaction. The sound

tickled my neck, and his chest vibrated against mine. Just so I could watch his face – watch his reaction - I pulled my head back to look at him as I ran my hand down his back and palmed his ass.

Then *he* moaned.

And *he* shuddered.

And it was me who laughed.

I'm not sure how many songs we danced like that... Grinding, swaying. Playing.

And I'd all but forgotten about being on film.

He breathed on my skin, his hands held me, his hip bone was teasing my cock. The music was loud and luring, the heat off his body, off other men, was consuming. The sway of the dance floor moved us. I could feel the bass beat in my chest.

I could also feel him. Oh fuck, could I feel him.

His long fingers clawed at me, his hands were so sure and demanding. He moved his hips, swaying with me, and as he pressed against me, needing friction. I could feel how turned on he was.

I turned in his arms and rubbed my ass against his hard-on. His fingers dug into my hips. His skin was so warm, his chest expanded against mine with every breath he took and I leaned my head back onto his shoulder and he moaned in my ear, "Mmmmm." He rubbed his dick against my ass. "Didn't think you'd like that?"

I smiled at his implied question. He wanted to know if I topped or bottomed. Chuckling, I turned around in his arms, melding our hips together and told him, "I am ambidextrous."

His eyes rolled closed and he groaned. I swear I could feel his cock twitch.

My Johnnie Walker-dulled senses didn't miss a fucking thing.

Unfortunately, Mr. Walker also sent words out of my mouth without being filtered first. "Fuck," I groaned. "You're so fucking hot."

His hands stalled on me, just a fraction, and his rhythm faltered. So I pulled my face back and looked into his eyes. They were slightly widened with surprise and vulnerability, but they were dark and deep with desire.

"It's true," I told him. I rolled my eyes playfully at him, "Like you don't know."

He blinked, and I realized it was a distinct possibility he truly didn't know how other men saw him. I shook my head and turned him so his back was pressed to my bare chest and his ass was against my cock. I spoke into his ear, "Look around, Cameron. All eyes are on you."

He did, and he could see it, how they looked at him, how they wished they were dancing with him, how they wished his hands were on them.

I leaned in, and my lips brushed his ear as I spoke. "Oh, how they wish they were me."

I spun him again so I could look at him. His cheeks were tinged with a pink that made his parted lips look red. Then fuck me, his tongue slid across his bottom lip.

I groaned. Loudly. "Oh, fuck," I said, looking away. "Don't do that."

So he sucked his bottom lip between his teeth. Was he trying to fucking kill me? My eyes closed, burning the image into my brain. I was still joined at the hip to him. I could feel how he was reacting to dancing with me. Surely, *surely* he could feel how hard my cock was.

I slid my hand around his jaw and my thumb pulled his lip from between his teeth.

I wondered if he knew how fucking close I was to kissing him right there.

I wanted to kiss him. I wanted to feel his lips against mine. I wanted his tongue in my mouth. I wanted to feel it, I wanted to know what he tasted like. I needed to know.

I needed to feel his lips, his tongue....

I needed... I needed....

...to do my job.

Dropping my hands from him, I took a deep breath and a step back. Ellie handed Cameron his phone. "You boys can dance for me anytime," she groaned, fanning her face dramatically with her hand. "Now, I need to find a man to put out this fire." She blew us both a kiss and shimmied away.

Before Cameron could speak, I led him off the dance floor to a quieter corner. Facing him, I reached down and readjusted my strangled hard-on, and Cameron couldn't disguise his surprise at my blatant admission to being aroused.

I shrugged. "You're fucking killing me out there," I nodded toward the dance floor.

I looked pointedly at his crotch... or more importantly, the all-too evident bulge in his jeans. "Killing you too, huh?"

Okay, so *that* made his jaw drop open.

"Come on," I smiled at him, leading him toward the exit. "That fucking clock you've got at home is ticking down without us."

CHAPTER SEVEN

I AM... IN-FUCKING-SANE

HE WAS quiet in the taxi from the club to his house, but he was wearing that scotch induced grin. We were both in the backseat of the cab, and I was grateful for the small distance between us. The fresh air seemed to have cleared my Cameron-fogged brain.

And the fresh air seemed to have hit Cameron hard. Who knew fresh, cool air mixed with six or seven shots of liquor made wobbly boots even wobblier? He swayed and fell against me, and I had had to help him into the taxi.

Now he was smiling and chuckling in little bursts.

"What's so funny?" I asked.

"Nothing," he giggled.

Fuck me. Cameron Fletcher just giggled.

"Tell me."

"Mm mm," he shook his head, then tried to read the time on his watch. He squinted and lifted his wrist to his face. "Whassatime?"

"Late," I told him. "Or early, rather. Time we were in bed."

His wide eyes grew even wider as he grinned and leaned toward me. "Really? Is that so?"

"You know what I mean."

"You shouldn't say things like that to me," he slurred. "S'been a while for me."

Holy shit.

Now it was my eyes that were wide, and my grin even wider, but the taxi driver interrupted us. "Hey! We're here."

I quickly threw the cabbie the fare, and helped Cameron out of the car. He probably could have stood on his own, but then I wouldn't have had an excuse to put my arm around his waist. And he wouldn't have had an excuse to have his arm around me.

We stumbled toward his front porch steps. "You alright there, champ?" I asked.

Cameron stopped walking. "Champ? Wha' the hell kinda name is that?"

"What would you like me to call you?" I asked. "Sport, mate, bud, dude..."

He straightened up and poked my chest. "Y'can call me the best you never had."

He laughed at my expression and pulled a key out of his pocket. I took it off him, figuring I had more of a chance of successfully getting the door unlocked and helped him up the stairs. I leaned him against the front door and stepped closer than could be considered polite.

"The best, huh?" I asked, my face just an inch from his.

He chuckled and nodded as his smile died. He looked at me with *that* look, I opened the door and he all but fell inside. I caught him before he hit the floor, kicked the front door shut and helped Cameron into the living room. I pushed him onto the sofa and dragged the coffee table over.

Sitting on it, I quickly pulled off my shoes and socks before I picked up Cameron's right foot and pulled off his shoe.

He looked at me. He didn't say a fucking word. He just lifted his left leg and dropped it onto my thigh, so I pulled that shoe off too.

And he was watching me. His head was resting on the back of the sofa, his eyes were fixed on my face. Slowly, he grinned.

Avoiding his stare, I looked down then, to his Sesame Street-striped feet. Fucking Bert and Ernie.

I hooked my fingers under the top of his sock and pulled it off too. "Sorry Bert, you gotta go." And then I did the same to the other foot. "You too, Ernie. Have fun in the wash, boys."

It made Cameron laugh.

And of course, then he wriggled his feet so I looked at them.

Fuck me.

Long, pale, and hairless. Beautiful bone structure, flawless arches, his toes were perfect.

Sweet baby Jesus, he had perfect toes.

I had to lick my lips and swallow, because my mouth was suddenly dry.

"Would you like a moment alone with them?" he asked, trying not to laugh. Funny bastard.

I stood up, letting his feet fall onto the coffee table, then leaned over and pushed him down until he was lying flat on his back. He gasped when I ran my hands over his hips until I found what I was looking for. I reached into his pocket and extracted his phone.

Holding it up, I grabbed his hand and pulled him back into a sitting position. "What did you think I was looking for, Cameron?" I asked suggestively. I turned the phone over in my hand and looked into his darkened eyes. "Leave my foot thing alone, anyway," I told him, "and I'll leave your sock thing alone."

He laughed and I sat down next to him.

Only, I didn't just sit *next* to him. I curled into him, right up close, laying my head on his chest, I pushed my feet against his. My left foot nudged his right foot, and my right foot rested on top of his.

Cameron froze, unsure of what to do. It was a little weird, granted. But it was a little bit fucking good, too.

I held up the phone and took some pictures of our feet. I moved my feet around a bit, trying to get different angles, but making it very clear these were two men in an intimate but not sexual position, just cuddling on the couch.

Too limited for shots in this position, I stood up and dragged Cameron into the kitchen with me. I could tell his buzz was starting to wane and fatigue was taking its place. "Just a few more," I said, knowing he wouldn't want to be this close to me in the light of day.

I pushed him against the kitchen counter and stepped between his legs. The angle wasn't as good, but the change of position was, for a few photos anyway. Cameron had his hands on my hips, and he leaned his forehead on my shoulder. I could feel the heat of his breath on my skin, and for a long moment, I forgot about the phone in my hand. All I could think about was him.

How close he was.

How he felt.

How he smelled.

I needed to reign in this want, this need. I was here to get a job done....

But I was standing in his kitchen, after a night of drinks

and dancing, pressing my hips into his, wanting to do so much more.

So. Much. More.

Cameron realized I'd stopped taking photos and lifted his head off my shoulder to stare at me. I knew he saw what I didn't want him to see. He could see it. He could feel it. I knew he could.

I wanted him.

Not only just *wanted*.

I was starting to actually *like* him.

Fuck.

He licked his lips and leaned forward, and I realized he was about to kiss me. And I panicked.

I wanted to. Fuck, I wanted to. But we needed to concentrate on work.

Before his lips met mine, I whispered, "Turn around."

His eyes fluttered closed and he swallowed, but he did it. Slowly, he turned around, so he was facing the counter, and his denim clad ass was in front of my cock. I wrapped my free hand around his waist and pulled him back into me.

Oh, fuck.

Somehow, I managed to take some photos of our feet. Well, I think I did. At least, I hoped that's what I did. He groaned, and with my hand, I pushed his shoulder down onto the kitchen bench.

I couldn't help it. I pushed against him almost roughly, so his heels left the floor as he leaned forward on his toes. With my feet between his in these photos, there was no mistaking our position.

Cameron groaned into the kitchen counter. "Oh, fuck."

I put the phone on the counter beside him and gripped the tops of his shoulders, pulling him upright. I whispered against the back of his neck. "Don't tempt me."

He moved so fast I barely saw it, but he turned to face me and with two strong hands and in two long strides, he'd pushed me up against the fridge. His chest was heaving, his eyes were dark and wild. I could feel his entire front against mine.

He was hard.

So was I.

His eyes flickered from my eyes to my lips, and I knew this was it. He was going to kiss me.

And I was going to let him.

He must have seen the consent in my eyes because then his lips were on mine. Silky, warm and wet, his lips opened and closed. This was no chaste first kiss.

He was demanding, urgent, and my mouth opened to taste him, to feel his tongue, to drink him.

Fuck.

Johnnie Walker and Cameron Fletcher.

His tongue invaded my mouth and all coherent thoughts were replaced with flashes of heat through my veins and gooseflesh.

My hands held his face, and I could feel his jaw working – opening and closing – as we kissed. Something in my brain was telling me to stop this.

But instead of pushing his mouth away, my hands held him tighter.

Instead of telling him we shouldn't be doing this, the only sounds I could make were moans.

Instead of resisting him, instead of stopping this kiss – this fucking delicious kiss – I kissed him harder.

He groaned, and right there, in his kitchen, up against his fridge, I wanted him. I wanted to feel him pulse in my hand, in my mouth. I want to taste his sweat. I wanted to taste his seed. I wanted to fuck him. I wanted him to fuck me.

I raked my hands down his chest, his ribs, to his hips, and I pulled him roughly into me, mashing our cocks together. I pulled my mouth from his, to breathe, to tell him what I wanted.

"Stop."

The word, though barely a breath, sounded loud, and definite.

And when he pulled away, with downcast eyes, I realized the word came from me.

He stepped away, his lips swollen, his breathing ragged and rejection written clear on his face.

"Cameron," I said, trying to get my breath.

He put his hand up to stop me, and he shook his head, taking another step away from me. "Don't."

I was quick to close the distance between us, and I grabbed his arm. He thought I'd rejected him. He was hurt. I had hurt him. "Look at me," I said. He did, but his eyes were guarded and defensive. I took his hand and held it against my hard-on. "Feel that?"

His eyes widened, but he gasped and nodded.

"Feel what you do to me?" I asked. "You have to know, Cameron, I *want* to... but not like this. Not drunk, not at three AM," I nodded pointedly to the other room. "And not with that fucking clock ticking down on us. We need to get this job done. We need to focus on that."

And I think he got it.

"I meant what I said tonight," I told him. "When this contract is a done deal, we'll go out again. When we're not working, we'll do this right."

His face fell. He looked down, but he nodded.

I touched his face, and my gesture made him look at me.

I leaned in and kissed his cheek. "Go to bed. I'll finish up down here."

He smiled, sort of, turned and walked out. I could hear him take the stairs, and then I was alone.

I had just turned down Cameron Fletcher.

I had just turned down Cameron Fucking Fletcher.

My cock was *aching*, and I had an ungodly urge to bang my head on the kitchen bench top. Maybe sleep deprivation and over-working led to in-fucking-sanity, because Lucas Hensley didn't turn down men like Cameron Fletcher.

Except I just did.

Flicking off the lights, I climbed the stairs, crawled into bed and tried not to think about what that meant.

CHAPTER EIGHT

I AM...REALLY FUCKING CONFUSED

I DIDN'T SLEEP. At all. Not one wink.

Normally, a few drinks send me out like a light. But not tonight. I ignored my protesting hard-on. My own cock hated me because I denied it some Cameron Fletcher.

Fuck.

I still didn't know why I stopped us. I knew, *I knew*, we were about two minutes from ripping off clothes and going at it. But I had to say stop.

The ache in my balls was my reward. I didn't bother jacking off. I relished the dull discomfort because it served me right.

What the fuck was I thinking?

Well, I knew what I was thinking... I was thinking I wanted to take my time with Cameron. I wanted to do it properly, not be just some quick fuck he'd regret. I was thinking I was starting to like him.

The realization made me groan.

What the fuck was I thinking?

This was Cameron Fletcher I was talking about here.

The man I worked with, who had ice in his veins. He was cold, distant and condescending.

Except he wasn't.

Not the guy I'd spent the last thirty-something hours with. The guy who was clever, funny, and had a thing for cartoon socks. The guy who was gay, sexy as hell, and who I just dry humped in his kitchen because I wanted him.

Yeah, that guy.

The guy who was still in the closet.

Him.

The one I couldn't stop thinking about.

Fuck.

Throwing back the covers, I threw on my jeans and a shirt. It was 4:30 AM, and if I wasn't sleeping, I might as well do some work. I found some Tylenol in the bathroom for the thump in my brain, headed downstairs, set the coffee machine dial to hurry-the-fuck-up, and made myself a brew strong enough to wake the dead.

I threw myself onto a chair at the dining table, took Cameron's phone and my laptop and got to work. First, was the footage of me doing the impromptu Q&A with the crowd at the nightclub, using Lurex supplies as bait. It was rough but it was real.

I wanted it unedited.

I wanted Lurex to hear what real gay men wanted, not some survey of folks telling other people what they thought they wanted to hear.

I loaded the footage onto my computer, saving it exactly as it was. It would need some editing, some cleaning up, but not much.

The next footage was of us dancing.

I saved the file onto my laptop first, and truthfully, I was nervous about watching it. I was hoping to use footage stills like photographs, to coincide – or to parallel – with footage of Ashley and Ben. Two couples in intimate positions, but not paying any preference to one couple over the other.

We would represent both couples as equals.

Because they were.

Except the couple on the dance floor weren't really a couple. It was me and Cameron. I had no idea what the footage even turned out like, but I was nervous about seeing us together. I was scared I might... like it.

I exhaled loudly and shook my tired head. And for some reason, I turned around to look at Cameron's countdown clock. Holy fucking shit.

29:12

We were down to twenty-nine fucking hours.

Suddenly, I didn't care about the nerves. I just hit play.

And I watched us. Ellie, our videographer extraordinaire, did an okay job. She managed to not get full face shots like I instructed, but she turned a little too quickly, or panned across us too fast. But that was easy enough to fix. I could slow it down, frame by frame if I had to.

The dance floor was darker than I remembered, and the strobing lights and noise made my head pound. I turned the sound down and adjusted the screen contrast to minimise the retina-burning lights.

And I watched two bodies dance and grind; one shirtless, one with a tight-fitting tee.

I watched wandering hands and fingers digging into skin. I watched as slender fingers skimmed the waistband of low-slung denim jeans, and I watched as familiar hands fisted into the back of the tee shirt. I watched hips grind and rock, and stomachs press together.

Then the bodies changed positions. Still moving, swaying, dancing, but now the naked chest pressed against the back of the grey fitted tee. Big hands wrapped around with wide spread fingers rubbing sides, abs.

My hands.

On Cameron.

Like that. Gripping, holding, scraping blunt fingertips across his stomach and my cock pressed against his ass, my chest against his back.

Fuck.

I wasn't watching some random, anonymous couple. I was watching us.

And we were fucking hot.

Then we swapped positions. I didn't really remember him behind me like that, but there it was on film, before my very eyes. His hips against my ass, his chest against my back. Long, pale fingers ran from my ribs to my thighs, Cameron's hands, on my body. Oh, that's right... when we were standing like that was when he whispered in my ear. That was when he basically asked me if I topped or bottomed....

I could see in the footage how hard I was. A fucking bulge in my jeans the size of my home state. God, I knew he had me hard on the dance floor, but to see it... And then, as if seeing it on the screen made me realize, I was acutely aware of the ache stirring in my cock. Fuck, even watching us was getting me hard.

I needed to focus. I couldn't jeopardize this contract because my fucking dick wouldn't behave. I could spend the rest of the week jerking off if I wanted to, and I probably would, but right here, right now, I needed to get this done.

I finished my coffee and got myself another one, deliberately not thinking about my dick. I thought about how pissed off – or worse, disappointed – Mr. Fletcher would be if we didn't get this deal. I thought about how disappointed

I would be if we didn't get this deal, and I could feel the ache dissipate. What it would mean for my job....

My dick didn't like the idea of failure, either.

Even as I watched the footage of us dancing twice more, my cock behaved. I lost the mindset of watching me with Cameron and focused on shots, angles and what could be digitally fixed and what couldn't. I cut it down, turned footage into stills, much like I did with the photographs of Ashley and Ben yesterday.

Thank fucking God for the digital age.

But then, *then*, I looked at the photos I took of Cameron's and my feet. There were no socks, his bare skin was on mine; his perfect feet on the coffee table, my legs draped over his, our feet tucked in together.

They were fucking beautiful.

I stared at the stills of our feet for ages, taking my time with each shot. Until I got to the pictures of us in the kitchen....

Holy.

Shit.

There were two photos, the angle was a little crooked, but they took my breath away. And made my dick hard. Again.

I was obviously standing behind Cameron, his feet faced the kitchen cabinet, spread wide, with my feet in between his. He was on his toes, his heels were off the ground, and my knees were slightly bent, pushing up into him.

If we were naked and fucking, I'd be so far inside him. I'd be thrusting up into him, reaching angles to make him groan, while bending him over the kitchen counter, fucking his ass....

But we weren't naked.

I adjusted my cock and palmed myself to relieve the pressure, but it only made it worse.

So I did it again, as I checked out how his feet looked with me standing between them. And I palmed my cock again, unable to look away from how the arches of his feet were perfect, how his toes were bent and he flexed so beautifully... how... oh, fuck.

I couldn't just rub one out sitting in Cameron's dining room. That would be just nasty.

But I groaned, knowing this erection wouldn't be ignored. I checked the time on Cameron's stupid clock.

27:30

I was too tired to work out what that was in real time. So I peeled off my shirt, and threw it at Cameron's stupid fucking clock, and checked the time on his phone instead.

6:30 AM. Perfect.

Morning shower time.

No sooner was the hot water running over my head, than I had my cock in my hand. It wasn't the tiles I saw, oh hell no. The images when I closed my eyes were of Cameron, and kitchen counters and feet and his bare ass and my cock buried deep inside him.

And it wasn't the slick body wash I used as lube in my fist to pump myself that felt slick and tight. It was Cameron's ass as I fucked him, feeding him every inch, fucking hard. His knuckles were white as he held on, and I rammed my cock into him. He was bent over the island bench, and he groaned and grunted and his ass squeezed my cock as he came....

Hard. I came so fucking hard, my knees almost gave out. The images in my mind of fucking Cameron made me shudder as my hand squeezed the last drops of come from my cock. I could still see him, in my mind's eye, how he'd writhed underneath me, riding out his orgasm with my own, his long, muscular body, sweaty and rippling with pleasure. My limp, heavy cock twitched one last time in my hand.

I became aware of the sounds of water and the heat of it on my skin as my senses came back to me. My eyelids were heavy, but I opened my eyes. I was spent. My orgasm had left me fucking tired. Tired, but relaxed, and if I had to spend the entire day working closely with Cameron, it was a good thing I'd just jerked off.

I dried myself, tied the towel around my waist and stepped out of the bathroom. Cameron's door was slightly open, and I tried not to peek inside. But of course, I couldn't help myself, so I did.

He was lying face down, his arms were raised up, under his pillow. I couldn't see his face, just the back of his head, but he was still sound asleep. He was probably gonna be pissed off at me for letting him sleep. Actually, he probably wouldn't be speaking to me after I stopped our dry-hump in the kitchen.

I had no idea how he'd react to me in the sober light of day or how awkward it would be between us. I left a sleeping Cameron, got dressed and went downstairs, wondering how our day would go. We had about twenty-seven hours left and if he wasn't speaking to me, then it was going to be a fucking long twenty-seven hours.

I wondered idly how much longer I should let him sleep, when his phone beeped.

I couldn't answer it. But I *could* look at the caller ID.

Mom.

I let the phone ring out, figuring his mother would leave a message, and he could call her back when he woke up. But then a message scrolled across his screen.

We're picking up breakfast. Will be there in 10.

I read it, and then I read it again.

We're picking up breakfast.

We're... as in *we are....*

Shit.

Mrs. Fletcher *and* Mr. Fletcher.

Cameron's dad, my boss, was gonna be here in ten fucking minutes.

I threw his phone on the table and raced upstairs, straight into his room. "Cameron!"

He turned and looked up, startled. "Wha? Huh?" His eyes took a moment to focus on me, and his head fell back onto the pillow with a groan. "...my head."

I laughed. "You don't have time to be hung over," I told him. "Your mom and dad will be here in nine minutes."

He buried his face into his pillow. "Mm mm."

I ripped the pillow off his face and pulled back the blanket to his waist. I caught a glimpse of underwear, so given he wasn't naked, I grabbed his hand and pulled him out of bed, toward the bathroom.

"What the fuck are you doing?" he protested.

I dragged him into the bathroom. "Your father is coming to check on the campaign. You need to at least look alive." I turned around, started the shower and then I turned back and looked at him.

Cameron. In his underwear.

His sculpted torso, defined abs and black briefs contrasted his pale skin perfectly. I could see the heavy outline of his cock through the dark material....

Fuck. Me.

I didn't even try to hide my ogling. He scrubbed his hands over his face, and when he opened his eyes, he stared at me. "You finished looking?"

"Not. Even. Close."

He looked at me, a mixture of hung over, amused and irritated. "Seven minutes..."

"Oh, I'll need longer than that with you..."

His mouth fell open. Then he added, "I meant until Dad gets here."

Oh, right. I grinned at him. "You only have five minutes to be showered, dressed and downstairs," I told him. "Don't shave. The stubble suits you," I told him. It was the truth, it did suit him. I got to the door and turned around to add, "And no jerking off. You don't have time."

His eyes narrowed. "Are you finished?"

"Oh, I finished jerking off in your shower about an hour ago."

And there I was thinking it was going to be awkward between us.

Smiling, I left him gaping at me, and went downstairs to get ready for the boss.

CHAPTER NINE

I AM... SHORT FUSED, HOT TEMPERED AND TOO FUCKING TIRED

27:12

By the time Cameron's parents arrived, I had most of the mess tidied up. I'd picked up our shoes from where we'd left them last night, and threw Bert and Ernie in the laundry. I'd tided the piles of paperwork without disturbing too much but made it look more organized, and I'd refilled the coffee machine.

When the doorbell chimed, I opened the door and was quite surprised by what I saw. It was Mr. Fletcher, and a woman I presumed to be Cameron's mother, except gone was the Armani suit and the superior disposition. The boss was wearing khaki slacks and a polo shirt, smiling and holding up a box of deli bags.

He chatted as he walked inside, heading straight for the kitchen, telling me how Cynthia insisted on Cameron's favorite pastries for breakfast, despite having to drive across town for them. She gently chided her husband, smiling at me as she did.

Mr. Fletcher was a different man. I mean, it was the

same man, except it wasn't. What was it with Fletcher men and their office personas?

"Lucas, I'd like you to meet Cameron's mother, my wife, Cynthia," Mr. Fletcher said warmly.

"Good morning, Ma'am," I said, tipping my imaginary hat, and Mrs. Fletcher smiled warmly at me.

I started pouring coffees just as Cameron walked into the kitchen. He smiled at his dad and kissed his mom's cheek. Knowing his pounding head was probably killing him, I handed him a coffee. I looked down at his feet, because well, I always looked at people's feet, and he was bare footed.

I looked from his perfect fucking feet to his perfect fucking face and smiled. He smiled back at me. It was a small, maybe teasing, maybe thankful smile but as his dad asked him something, I saw Mrs. Fletcher was looking at the exchange between her son and me. She grinned at me with knowing in her eyes.

She knew.

She knew. Ashley knew. Simona knew. The only ones who didn't know were Cameron's brother and father.

The men.

Diverting her attention, I asked her, "Coffee, Mrs. Fletcher?"

"Oh yes Dear, please. And Lucas, please call me Cynthia."

I smiled at her. "Sorry Ma'am, but my Momma would be on the first plane to Chicago to tan my hide if I ever called a lady by her given name."

She giggled, and I noticed then, Mr. Fletcher and Cameron were both watching us. The father was smiling, and the son was a little perplexed, I think, that I was making his mother laugh.

I handed a smiling Mr. Fletcher his coffee, and offered sugar and cream to Mrs. Fletcher. She, in turn, offered us the selection of pastries they had brought with them.

And then Mr. Fletcher asked the twenty million dollar question. "So, what are you taking to Lurex?"

I looked at Cameron, and I could see he was stuck. Because by telling his father what avenue we were taking, by showing him what photos we'd taken and what footage we had, in the form it was right now, he'd be giving more than our campaign away.

He'd be coming out.

So I answered for him. "If it's okay with you, Cameron, I'd rather not say right now."

Both men looked at me; Cameron was relieved, his father surprised and curious. I didn't want to piss Mr. Fletcher off, or undermine his intelligence, so I explained, "At the moment, it's an unedited and a raw product, and I don't want you to think we're not on schedule. We are, but it still needs pulling together."

Mr. Fletcher frowned. "Is there anything I can do to help?"

"Yes," I nodded as I sipped my coffee. "We'll need access to the art and graphics department at Head Office at around four this afternoon."

"Okay," he nodded seriously. "No problem. I can organize that." He seemed happier now that he was contributing something. "You boys look tired. The sun's out, we should sit outside so you two can get some sunshine."

With that, we took our coffees and pastries and went out to the back patio. I didn't even know Cameron had a patio. Sitting at the outdoor setting, I had to admit, the sun felt good. My head fell back and the sun on my face warmed my skin.

Mr. Fletcher's voice kept me from falling asleep. "Miss the Texas sun?"

My eyes opened reluctantly, and I looked at him. "Mmm, sometimes," I admitted, somewhat sleepily.

"Jesus, Lucas," Cameron's father huffed. "Have you slept at all?"

I smiled. "Not last night, no."

Cameron stared at me. I looked at his father and explained, "Got a lot on my mind." I deliberately didn't look at Cameron, even though I could feel his eyes on me, and finished my coffee. "I can sleep tomorrow, after the meeting."

Mrs. Fletcher clucked her tongue at me, just like my Momma did, and Mr. Fletcher narrowed his eyes at me, then at his son. "Cameron, make sure he gets *some* sleep. Put him to bed yourself if you have to."

Cameron coughed, almost choking on his bagel, and mumbled something I couldn't make out.

Mrs. Fletcher changed the topic, saving her son from further embarrassment. "So, Tobias told me it's a big contract deal?"

I smiled and nodded, and she pressed the issue, "Tell me, what has my dear husband got you two boys working all weekend for? Lurex, isn't it?"

I answered her honestly. "Yes, Ma'am. Condoms and lube – ah, personal lubrication, Ma'am."

Cameron's eyes popped and he stared at me. Mrs. Fletcher leaned over and pats his arm. "It's okay, Cameron. Condoms or cornflakes, it's just another product."

He rolled his eyes. "I know that, Mom."

"So, tell me," she said, sipping her coffee with a smile. "How *do* you go about researching their products?"

I smiled at her, but Cameron answered first. "Firstly, we

look at markets, trends, sales percentages, target research... you know, condoms or cornflakes, it's all the same, just another product."

She looked at him, he grinned at her, and she laughed. Mr. Fletcher shook his head at them.

Cameron's mother's smile faded. "Except not having cornflakes, as opposed to condoms, won't change the course of your life," she said softly. Then she explained, "I do some volunteer work at the local respite house for people living with HIV... Sometimes it doesn't cost you the price of a condom. Sometimes it costs you a whole lot more."

Mr. Fletcher started talking about the funding for the respite house, but I wasn't paying much attention. I was looking at Cameron. I could see his *I'm thinking* face, but all I could do was try not to yawn. Standing up, I thanked Cameron's parents for breakfast, citing the need to get back to work, but truthfully, the warmth of the sun was putting me to sleep.

Back inside, I poured myself another coffee, trying to wake myself up. Cameron chatted with his parents for a few minutes, and not long after, they came inside to say good-bye. When Mrs. Fletcher said it was a pleasure to meet me, I tipped my invisible hat and told her, "The pleasure was mine, Ma'am."

She beamed at the gesture, Cameron rolled his eyes at me and Mr. Fletcher grinned.

When Cameron's parents had gone, he came straight into the kitchen. "You didn't go to sleep at all? Did you work *all* night?" I couldn't tell whether he was pissed off or concerned.

I shook my head at him. "No, I *tried* to go to sleep. I was a bit distracted by our encounter in your kitchen."

"Oh." He sighed and ran his hands through his hair,

leaning against the counter next to me. Before I could worry too much about it being awkward between us, he sighed again. "Thank you."

I looked at him, raising a questioning eyebrow. "What for?"

"For waking me up," he said. "My father would have been *pissed* if he got here and I was asleep and you were working."

"I would have covered for you," I told him.

He huffed and smiled before rubbing his temples. "How did you know they were on their way?"

"I had your phone connected to my laptop, working on the footage and the photos," I told him. "I didn't answer it, I swear. I saw it was your Mom's number, and then a text message scrolled across your screen saying they'd be here in ten minutes."

He nodded. "S'okay. Thanks anyway."

I looked down at the floor in front of us and could see his beautiful bare feet poking out from beneath his jeans. I tapped my socked foot on his bare one and smiled at him.

"Teasing me with bare feet, huh?"

He chuckled. "For the comment you left me with in the bathroom."

Oh, that's right. I told him I jerked off in his shower. I smiled and shrugged without shame. "Well, watching footage of us dancing was bad enough, but then I saw the photos of our feet...."

He swallowed thickly, groaned and shook his head. "Um... how... how did they turn out?"

"Have a look," I said, smiling. I walked through to the dining table and opened my laptop. I started the unedited footage of us dancing first.

I didn't watch the screen. I watched him.

His eyes were wide, and he swallowed several times. When it was finished, "Jesus..." was all he could say.

I grinned at him and then started the slideshow of foot pictures. The screen stopped on the last one. The one of us in the kitchen with him on his toes bent over, and me behind him, grinding my cock against his ass and pushing him into the kitchen counter.

He looked at me and swallowed. His eyes were wide and dark, and he licked his lips.

I tapped the laptop screen. "Hence my need to jack off in the shower."

He nodded, and I chuckled. But he was looking at the pictures and his brow furrowed. "Thank you... for not letting Dad see these. He'd know it was us... me." He swallowed, then whispered, "Oh, God. He's going to know it's me."

I looked at him then; his eyes were downcast. "Hey," I said, making him look at me. "I'll show you what I started to do with the footage and photos. I promise you, when it's done, he'll never know."

He nodded and gave me a sad smile. I showed him what I started on in the early hours of the morning. He could see which direction I was going, where I wanted the pictures to go. I explained, "Having done the ones of Ashley and Ben yesterday, it's really just a matter of finding the ones of us that match best."

He nodded. "These are good," he said.

"Of course they are." I rolled my eyes at him, trying to get him to smile. It worked. But then I yawned.

"You should go lie down for a while," he said quietly.

I tried to object but only yawned again. "Will you wake me up in me three hours?"

"Four."

I rolled my eyes, and he smiled. "I'll keep going with these," he said. "I'll wake you at...." He looked at his count-down clock, which had my shirt thrown over it, then he looked at me.

"It annoyed me," I told him with a pout.

He smiled. "I'll wake you in four hours."

I nodded and trudged my tired ass up the stairs, peeling my shirt off as I went. The shirt fell on the floor near my bag, and I fell onto the bed. I didn't bother taking my jeans off, and I didn't bother pulling back the covers.

I don't even remember falling asleep.

22:35

The next thing I knew there was a God awful buzzing noise somewhere near my head. Stupid fucking buzzing noise. My hands reached blindly, trying to shut it up, and I found it. It was my phone. On the pillow. Near my head.

The alarm on my phone had been set to go off. I didn't set it....

Cameron. Cameron must have set it. And come into the room while I was sleeping to place it on the pillow near my head.

Nice way to come and wake me up, asshole. I grabbed my phone, and not bothering to put on a shirt, trudged back down stairs to thank him personally. I didn't expect to wake to a string quartet harping out Mozart, but Jesus H Christ... a fucking phone alarm in my ear impersonating a jack-hammer wasn't exactly pleasant.

I hadn't woken up in a very good mood, but that wasn't the fucking point. I never wake up in a good mood, but that's not the fucking point either.

I stomped down the stairs, through the hall and into the living room. "Cameron!" But he wasn't there. So I stomped into the kitchen, and he wasn't there either. "Cameron!"

No answer. Fuck.

Actually, the house was quiet. Too quiet.

Cameron wasn't anywhere.

Just before my blood could boil, my phone buzzed in my hand. Caller ID flashed his name.

Cameron.

I didn't bother with pleasantries. I answered his call, "Where. The fuck. Are you?"

CHAPTER TEN

I AM NOT A HAPPY CAMPER

"UH... PARDON?"

"I said, where the fuck are you?"

Silence.

I checked my phone to see if the line had been disconnected. It wasn't. He was still there. "So," I fucking hated repeating myself, "where are you? And thank you *very fucking much* for waking me up."

I took a deep breath. I knew I was being unreasonable and a little – or a lot - immature, so I tried exhaling slowly to calm the fuck down.

"I set your alarm," he hissed through the phone. I could just picture him with his jaw clenched as he spoke. "And I'm calling you now to make sure you didn't sleep through it. I finished editing what I could of the photos, *thank you very fucking much*, and decided to add something to the campaign - which I'll show you when I get back. Right now, if you really must know, I'm standing in a line at the deli. I was going to ask you whether you liked ham or chicken in your salad, but you can get yourself something to eat, *thank you very fucking much*."

The line clicked in my ear. *Now* the line was disconnected.

Fuck, fuck, fuck.

I threw my phone on the table, even more pissed off than I was five minutes ago. *Now* I was pissed off because I'd had seven hours sleep in the last two days, I was pissed off because he had apparently finished the raw editing the photos already, *and* he had decided to add something to the campaign without checking with me – or waking me.

But more than anything, I was pissed off because now... *now* I had to apologize for being an ass.

Resisting the urge to scream, I pulled at my hair, took another deep breath and counted to ten. First in English, then in Spanish.

And then in French.

When I'd calmed down enough, I opened up my laptop and looked through what he had done.

Now I felt like even more of an ass.

He had finished doing what I started, using my ideas, just like I showed him. They were perfect.

Now we had almost identical shots of a straight couple and a same-sex couple. Same poses, same positions, body shots, with Ben's front and Ashley's fingertips down the waistband of his jeans, then me and Cameron on the dance floor. I was shirtless, and he was behind me with his hands on my stomach, his fingertips skimming inside my jeans.

Then the photos of our feet; he'd gone with the one of Ben and Ashley standing, her foot edging up the hem of Ben's jeans. And he'd used the one of us, standing in his kitchen – the one where we were facing each other – but it was different. It took me a second to realize he'd mirror reversed the image, making our pose match Ashley and Ben's.

Very clever, Cameron. Very clever.

Now we just needed to do a final edit, get them onto visual display boards, and get the video footage edited properly, all of which we needed to go into Head Office for. I looked at Cameron's countdown clock.

21:47

By my calculations, we should be able to pull this off. And maybe, just maybe, I'd be able to go home and sleep for a full six hours. Excited by the idea, I looked around at what shit of mine I could pack up to take home.

I picked up my boots, my jacket and the second brown paper bag of Lurex goodies, the one with the dildos, probes and cock rings.

Walking upstairs, I figured I wasn't entitled to *all* of them, so I tipped them out onto the bed and halved them. I re-packed Cameron's half into the brown paper bag and left them in his bathroom, then shoved mine into my overnight bag, packing whatever else I could. I stripped the bed, figuring I wouldn't be needing it tonight, and took the armful of linen downstairs just as Cameron walked through the front door.

He eyed me, but said nothing, and walked through the doorway to the living room.

I followed him through to the kitchen and dumped the dirty linen in the laundry.

He put one of two takeaway containers on the kitchen bench. "I take it you've decided not to stay another night."

I shook my head in agreement. "We should be done," I told him. "If we head into work in an hour or so, I figure we can get it wrapped up tonight and I can just go home after we were done."

His brows furrowed and with a frown, he nodded.

"Cameron, I'm sorry," I told him. "For the way I spoke to

you on the phone. I don't have any excuse. I was an ass, and I'm sorry."

His eyebrow lifted a little, and he simply pushed the takeaway container toward me. "I got you ham salad. If you don't like it, too bad." And with that, he walked away.

So, I guess my apology wasn't accepted.

Fuck.

I picked up the salad container. "Thanks," I said, loud enough for him to hear. He didn't respond, and I pretended I didn't care.

He was back to being Mr. Fucking Impossible, Mr. Hot and Cold, and I was too tired to give a fuck.

And there I was starting to like the guy. Not just *like* as in a-work-colleague kind of way, but like in a I-want-to-get-to-know-him kind of way. Sure, he was hot, but he was also intelligent, and he was intriguing. He was also sitting in the other room like I didn't exist and as though my apology didn't mean shit.

I stood at the kitchen counter and ate the lunch he brought me, wondering where that left me.

Not just with him, but at the company. If we got the Lurex contract, it'd be all sunshine and roses, but if we didn't? Well, I would imagine a little restructuring would be in order. If the two top executives simply couldn't work together, then one would have to go.

And rest assured, Mr. Fletcher wasn't about to fire his son.

So, that left me.

I was suddenly not very hungry. Actually, there was a great big fucking lump in my stomach. I pushed the container away and, leaning my elbows on the countertop, I buried my face in my hands.

How the fuck did I get here?

Forty-something fucking hours ago, I went to work, all buzzed for a Friday. Then I was placed under house arrest with the one man who I thought never liked me; the same man who turned out to be a closeted gay man; the same man, the very same man who kissed me, who I kissed back, who I damn near dry-humped in this very kitchen.

Because I wanted him.

And, if I was honest with myself, because I wanted him still.

Fuck.

"Are you okay?" His voice startled me.

I looked up. *Am I okay?* No, no I wasn't. "Yep," I lied. "Good as gold."

"You didn't eat much."

I shrugged. "Thanks for getting it for me anyway. You didn't have to do that."

He put his empty container in the trash. "Do you want to see what I did when I went out?"

Oh, I'd forgotten about that. He said he did something for the campaign. He was trying to be nice, so I tried to smile. "Sure."

It was different between us now. I knew he was tired. I was too. But apart from the dark circles under his eyes, there was a sadness. A resignation. A finality. Whatever hope there was for something between us, be it a professional or personal relationship, was gone.

He trusted me with his secret. He kissed me... and I said stop. He'd decided I wasn't worth the risk, and my yelling at him at the phone only reinforced his decision.

He hooked up a hand-held recorder to his laptop and pressed play. What he showed me stopped me in my tracks.

"My mom said something that got me thinking," he

explained coolly. "She made the comment about the price of a condom and how it can cost a life...."

I remembered when she said that, and I remembered looking at Cameron, wondering what he was thinking. Then I remembered trying not to fall asleep in the sun.

"The campaign concept has been all yours so far," he added, so matter of fact. "This is my contribution." He pressed play.

The footage was unedited, as real as it can possibly be. A lady, once possibly beautiful, sat with a blanket over her lap. But it was Cameron's voice which sounds on-screen first. "Just start with your name," he prompted.

The lady smiled, though her ingrained sorrow remained. "My name is Amy," she said. "I was diagnosed with HIV four years ago. I had unprotected sex..." her voice trailed away.

"I was young, thought 'that can't happen to me'." She looked off camera and coughed.

Cameron waited patiently before his voice asked, "How much did it cost you?"

She smiled without humor. "Everything."

The footage cut then, and the on-film Cameron sat down beside a man. "My name is James," the man said. "I'm HIV positive. Been here for 12 months now," he added, looking around the room. "Treat me real nice here, they do."

On the footage, Cameron's voice said, "How much does your medication and treatment cost you a month?"

James answered, "I don't got no benefits... just for my meds, about a hundred bucks every month."

I watched the footage, unblinking. When it finished, I looked across. He was watching me, waiting for my reaction. "Cameron, it was..." my voice was quiet as I tried to find the right word. "...it's brilliant."

He nodded once, closed down his laptop and stood up. "Right. If you're ready, we'd better head into the office," he said, almost robotically. He started packing up folders and putting them into the archive boxes. "If we're adding this new aspect to the campaign, we need to move. We'll be lucky to get it done in time."

I looked at the clock.

20:56.

Fuck.

Two minutes later, I had my jacket and boots on, loaded everything we needed into Cameron's car and we were on our way into Head Office. He still wouldn't look at me. I tried to coax conversation out of him, but his answers were sharp and short.

I tried *not* to get annoyed. I tried *not* to let him get to me.

But he *did* get to me.

He got right in under my skin.

The more he didn't say, the more he ignored me, the more he fucking *dismissed* me, the more he got to me.

And by the time we'd hauled our workloads out of the car and into the elevator at work, he was right back to being the arrogant, supercilious prick I'd known over the last six months. He stepped away, keeping a distance between us, and when we stepped out of the elevator onto our floor, it was as though I was nothing more than a stranger to him.

Well, fuck that.

And fuck him.

Because my arms were full, I used my foot to open my office door and slammed it closed behind me with a satisfying kick. I dumped the boxes onto my desk with a loud thump, and I knew he could see me through the glass walls between us.

But I. Didn't give. A fuck.

Let him see me pacing, let him watch me pull at my fucking hair, let him see me taking deep breaths trying to calm the fuck down.

He was all cool, calm and collected, like he had some special self-control switch he could turn off and on. Whereas, I didn't. I wore my emotions on my fucking sleeve for the world to fucking see, and he was all unruffled.

Needing to focus my energy, I grabbed my laptop satchel and stomped back out to the elevator. I pressed the button for Floor 18 just as Cameron stepped out into the hall and walked toward the elevator.

Oh, you are fucking kidding me.

Of course he was heading to the arts and graphics department with me. Of course he had to get into the elevator with me. Of course he did. Of course the doors didn't close before he got here. Of course the doors would wait for Cameron Fucking Fletcher to walk inside before closing. Stupid fucking elevator. Of course he still didn't look at me. Of course he didn't acknowledge me.

Inhale.

One, two, three, four, five, six, seven, eight, nine, ten.

Exhale.

Uno, dos, tres, cuatro, cinco, seis, siete, ocho, nueve, diez.

Inhale.

Un, deux, trois, quatre, cinq, six, sept, huit, neuf, dix.

Exhale.

The doors opened, and without a word, without even so much as a glance, he stepped out before me.

Floor 18 was a large open space. There were several work stations across the floor, each consisting of its own drawing table and graphics computer with a hub of printing machines along the back wall. It was what I'd imagine if you put a student art room, a state of the art IT room and a printing press all in one room would look like.

Cameron took an immediate left, and I went right. I started working on finalizing the photos, and he started working, from scratch, on his footage. And because he was acting like I wasn't even in the same room as him, I pulled out my phone, plugged in my earphones, scrolled through playlists until I found 'workout' and pressed play. Loud, pumping music filled my brain, distracting me from all things Cameron.

But he was sitting at a table across the room, in a clear line of sight.

I tried not to watch him. I tried not to look at his ass in those jeans, how he sat on that stool, or how the denim hugged his thighs. I tried not to watch his back in that shirt, how broad his shoulders were, how defined his waist was. I tried not to think about him, how he looked without the shirt....

I didn't notice how many times he ran his hand through his hair. I didn't notice how he spun a pen through his long fingers. I didn't notice his jaw, and I didn't count how many times he licked his lips.

And I didn't, I really didn't notice his feet. I tried really, really hard to not wonder what kind of funny socks he was wearing.

I turned my back to him, and the music helped me focus on the task at hand. Soon enough, I was lost in my work as I continued with the editing and perfecting of the photos, footage and my little impromptu Q&A at the nightclub. I had no fucking idea what the time was, or how long I'd been sitting at that desk, but when I looked up, the Chicago skyline was illuminated by night, and Cameron was not at his desk.

The room was empty, and I pulled out my earphones to find it was also very quiet.

I checked the time on my phone. It was 8:17pm.

Fuck. The meeting was in 13 hours and 43 minutes.

I slid off the stool, stiff and sore, aching in parts of my body that strictly shouldn't ache.

I needed coffee.

Because the design room has a strict no food, no drink policy, I headed back up to my office, knowing there was always coffee there. As soon as the elevator doors opened, I heard him.

I knew it was him, because there wasn't a sound in the world like it.

Cameron was laughing.

I didn't know whether to be curious or cranky. So I settled on both.

Then I heard other voices, and when I walked into the staff room, he was there. He was talking to the cleaning staff, a man and a woman he called Gustavo and Maria, and they were speaking in Spanish.

They stopped talking when I walked in. "Don't mind me," I told them. "Just want coffee." I set about making myself a straight black, and as I was waiting for the water to boil, their conversation resumed.

Once again, like I wasn't even there.

And my already thin patience started to crack. I tried not to eavesdrop, but then I heard my name.

"Across the hall from me," Cameron said quietly in Spanish to Maria. And I knew then he was talking about me.

"Ah, si," the older lady said. "The new boy. You like working with him?" she questioned him in Spanish.

Cameron hesitated, but answered, still speaking in Spanish. "Very much. He's very good at what he does."

I could feel my patience and my temper stretch tight and I turned around to face them. "That's me," I said in Spanish. "Selling the unsellable."

Cameron's face paled, whether at me speaking Spanish, or because I repeated his very words back. I smiled at Cameron, well, it was probably more of a sneer, and after one glance between us, Gustavo and Maria quietly disappeared out the door.

I stared at Cameron, and he stared at me. I almost snarled when I spoke. "If you want to say something to me, Cameron, then fucking say it in English. And say it. To. Me."

He gritted his teeth. "Gustavo and Maria don't speak English very well. They've worked for my father since I was a kid. I will speak with them however the hell I want."

He stormed out of the room and slammed his office door behind him.

And my patience finally fucking snapped. It was too bad Gustavo and Maria left, because if they hadn't, they could have learned some four letter words in English.

I followed him down the hall, ripped open his office door and he spun around to look at me.

And I let him fucking have it. "What. The *fuck*. Is your problem?"

CHAPTER ELEVEN

I AM...NOT SO FRUSTRATED ANYMORE

"GET *OUT* OF MY OFFICE." Cameron glared at me, and when he took a deep, calming breath, I thought I might have just scratched his Mr. Nothing-Phases-Me veneer exterior.

My Hensley-Texas temper was frayed, I was fucking tired and he'd gotten under my skin, only to then dismiss me. I was at breaking point with this man. Something had to give.

"No."

He clenched his jaw and hissed at me through clench teeth. "Lucas-"

I cut him off. "Don't you *dare* dismiss me, Cameron. Don't act like I mean nothing." I took a step toward him and pointed my finger at him. "Don't. You. Fucking. Dare."

He glared at me, his eyes were wild, and I could tell I was getting to him. I was getting under his skin. I could feel it.

"I'm sorry I yelled at you," I told him, trying to stay calm. "I'm sorry I hurt you. I know you put yourself out there, you took a chance. You kissed me, Cameron. You *finally* come out to someone, and when you kissed them, they told you to stop."

"That's not it," he said.

"Bullshit, Cameron," I countered quickly. "I saw how much I hurt you. You've been distant from me since. You won't talk to me. You won't look at me."

"That's not why," he answered quietly.

"Then why?" I yelled at him. "Tell me fucking why, Cameron! For the last forty-something fucking hours you've been open, funny and warm. I've seen the real you. I finally think, hey I could see myself with a guy like you."

That made him look at me.

"You were there last night, Cameron. You weren't *that* drunk – don't tell me you didn't feel it. How hot it was between us, when we danced, when we kissed." I took a deep breath and admitted, "I didn't *want* to stop..."

He shook his head and stared straight at me. "Then why did you?"

"This fucking job," I almost yelled at him. "This fucking campaign."

He stopped at my words like they hurt him. "The job..." he shook his head. "It's all about the fucking job to you, isn't it?"

"No!" I barked at him, so fucking frustrated. Even pulling at my hair didn't help. "No, this," I indicated between us, "isn't just about the God*damn* job, Cameron. But if we don't get this contract, my ass'll be thrown on the next fucking plane to Texas."

Confusion flickered across his face. "What the hell are you talking about?"

"If we can't work together, if we fail, do you think your father will still want me here?" I asked him. "*That's* what I'm talking about."

"He wouldn't do that," he cried, shaking his head.

"Why the hell wouldn't he?"

"Because I wouldn't let him!" he yelled at me so loud, the veins in his neck stood out. "That's why!" He cried, throwing his hands up. "Godammit Lucas, you've been all I can fucking think about for the last four months. I've tried to forget about you. I tried to ignore you. I've tried to *not* want you."

He stepped closer to me. "You are who you are, no excuses. Professional, fucking brilliant at your job and *out*! You're fucking *out*!" He thumped his hands at his chest. "And what am I? A fucking coward."

I was stunned by his admission. My mouth fell open as he continued his rant. "Then spending all this time with you only makes me want you more. We danced. And we kissed. In my kitchen! God," he groaned. "I would have gone to bed with you if you hadn't stopped me. I would have let you fuck me."

A shiver rippled from the back of my head, down my spine, propelling me forward. There was no conscious decision to cross the distance between us. My body just moved.

My hands grabbed his face, I pulled our mouths together and I kissed him. It wasn't polite, and it wasn't sweet. It was *want* and *need* and frenzy and deep. He froze against me, for just a moment, surprised by my sudden attack.

But as my tongue met his, I could feel him melt into me and as soon as he gave in, I pushed him back against his desk.

My hands were still holding his face, holding his mouth in place as I fucked it with my tongue. My body pushed against his, hard and rough. Then his hands were on me, pushing me, holding me, gripping me.

He had nowhere to go. His ass was against his desk and I was pressing him into it. My hips were pinning him there, my hardened cock against his. Hot, hard, aching.

He said he'd wanted me for four months.

I was all he could think about.

He said he would have gone to bed with me.

He would have let me fuck him.

The thought of it made me groan – having him underneath me, being inside him, feeling my cock in his ass, his heat, how he'd pulse around me, how he'd make me come.

Ripping my mouth from his and pulling my hips from his, my entire body shuddered.

His lips were red and swollen, and his eyes took a moment to open and focus. And for a brief moment, he thought I was going to reject him again. I could see the fear in his eyes.

"Cameron... you're..." I tried to tell him, while trying to control my body, my breathing. "You're gonna make me come."

He exhaled and grinned, and his hands were on my fly, ripping my jeans open. His fingers dipped in under my briefs, and his hand wrapped around my cock, making me hiss.

"Jesus..."

He pulled me out, exposing me to him. He looked from the engorged dick in his hand to my eyes, and he groaned. "Please."

I couldn't stop him, even if I'd wanted to. I groaned, I hissed, I thrust my cock into his hand and I begged. "Ohgodplease, please, please."

He plunged his mouth onto mine and pumped me, hard, fast and so, so good. He slid his hand, gripping and twisting and I knew this was it... this was it.

Fuck, this was it.

Pulling my mouth from his, I tried to warn him. But he seemed to understand, because he squeezed me harder, pumped me, thrust his hips into me, and against my lips, he whispered, "Show me."

Then he watched me come.

Heat ripped right through me, from my toes and my scalp and surges in thick, short bursts. My cock erupted, hot and pulsing, as long fingers continued to squeeze me, and I was lost. I was lost to everything but him, there was no sight, no sound, only him. His hand still held me, his body pressed against mine, my head on his shoulder, how he felt, how he smelled.

How I smelled on him.

Finally, my eyes opened drunkenly, and I looked at him. He stared at me in wonder. I looked down between us, to my come on his hand, on my stomach and staining my shirt. I pulled the soiled tee-shirt over my head, and before I could offer to wipe his hand, he lifted his hand to his mouth and his pink tongue licked my come off his skin.

I moaned at the sight, and he moaned at the taste, his other hand palmed the bulge in his pants. He was still resting against his desk, so I grabbed the button fly on his jeans and pulled them open. "You've tasted me," I rasped out. "Now let me taste you."

Tucking myself back into my briefs, I fell to my knees. I looked up at him, his eyes were wide, but dark and glazed. I pulled the material of his briefs down, letting his swollen cock spring free.

Oh, fuck.

I grabbed his hips and licked his entire length, his long, oh-so long shaft and leaking slit... oh, fuck. My mouth watered and I groaned, but my lips opened to take him, to taste him.

"Fuck!" he groaned. He bucked his hips, and his hands held my face as his cock slid in and out of my mouth. I worked him, sucking and licking. His grip on my hair tightened and his hips jerked in short bucks. "Fuck, fuck," he huffed.

I pumped the base of his shaft with one hand and cupped his balls with the other. He held my head tighter and fucked my throat deeper.

I moaned to tell him I liked it.

His hands slipped from my hair, and he held my face, my jaw, my neck. I moaned again and he could feel the vibrations on his fingers and on his cock, and he flexed one last time before he came.

Cameron growled out a guttural sound as he swelled and exploded in my mouth. I swallowed and drank him down, every spurt, hot and thick. His whole body trembled as I licked him and let him go from my mouth, tucking him back into his pants. And when I stood up, he slid off the table into me. I wrapped my arms around him, catching him, and I chuckled when he whimpered. We stood like that for a few too-short minutes, catching our breaths.

"Fuck," he whispered against my neck.

"Mmmm," I hummed against his ear. "I'd like to. But I'll need at least ten minutes to recover."

He huffed out a chuckle, his breath was hot on my skin. But then he pushed me away, pulling himself from me. He walked to the far wall, but his eyes were downcast, whether shy or regretful, I just didn't know.

Shirtless, I stepped back to give him the room he needed and I did up my fly. My shirt was a soggy mess on the floor and as I was wondering if I should hand wash it, or how long it would take to dry, Cameron said, "Um, this should fit you."

He was standing near his personal bathroom and holding a shirt on a hanger. "I keep spare business shirts. In case of emergencies."

Emergencies? "Do you expect to have jizz on your shirt often?"

He rolled his eyes. "In case I spill coffee."

Oh.

I smiled and shrugged, and he gave me a half a grin. I took the shirt, slipped it on and buttoned it and started rolling the sleeves up while Cameron straightened up his jeans.

"We'd better get back to work," he said, still somewhat hesitant.

"Cameron," I said his name to stop him. "What we just did," I motioned toward his desk, "well, that's something I'd like to do again. I meant what I said about taking you out and doing this right."

He seemed to frown, but he nodded... sort of.

Shit.

"Unless, you don't want to," I said, offering him a get-out-of-jail-free card.

"Lucas," he whispered. He looked at me with his imploring hazel eyes. "I do want to, but..."

"But what?"

"You won't want me. I'm... I'm not out. I don't expect you, or any man, to step back into the closet for me."

I smiled and walked right up to him so I could trace my fingers down the side of his jaw. "And I don't expect any man to out himself, before he's ready, for me. It's something you need to do in your own time, on your own terms."

He looked at me seriously for a moment, then he

nodded. "Thank you," he said with a sad smile. "I want to. I want to be out. I want to be free to be myself. I'm so sick of hiding..."

"I know," I nodded, because I did know. I knew *exactly* what he meant. "When you're ready. But we can still hang out, yeah? Go out for dinner, drinks...?"

"I'd like that," he grinned and nodded, so I kissed him. It was a soft, make-out kind of kiss. His whole face shone and a light pink tinted his cheeks. Fuck me, I think we just made ourselves an official date.

"Is that a date?" I asked with another peck to his lips, just to clarify.

He chuckled. "Maybe."

"Oh, I see," I joked, walking to his door, holding it open for him. "Come on, Mr. Playing-hard-to-get, we need to get back to work."

"Hard to get?" he asked, incredulously. "After what we just did?"

I laughed. "Well, hard maybe..." I stopped him in the empty hall. "Cameron, can I ask you something?"

He stopped at my serious tone, a little worried about what was on my mind.

"It's been killing me, I need to know. Who's on your socks today?"

He grinned. "The Lone Ranger and Kimosabe."

"Of course it is." I rolled my eyes and laughed. "I bet it took a while to find that pair."

"You have no idea," he laughed, then and when we stepped into the elevator, he pressed the button for the ground floor.

"Where are we going?" I asked.

"To get some proper coffee and some dinner." He grinned. "I'm starving."

"Anyway," I reminded him, "don't you mean Tonto?"

Still grinning, he nudged me with his elbow. "Shut the fuck up."

10:26

We grabbed some pizza and espresso, deciding to eat at the pizzeria, knowing we couldn't take food back into the design room. And he was back, the Cameron that laughed and joked, chatted and talked openly. He told me he meant what he said, he'd wanted me for months. He wanted so bad to have the courage to say something, anything.

He told me with a shrug that when he saw me walking down the stairs with the stripped bed linen, he knew I'd decided to leave. His brow furrowed when he said it shouldn't have surprised him. After all, why on Earth would an out-and-proud gay man want to stay with a closeted man?

I told him a real man, the right man, would wait.

He looked at me, really, *really* looked at me and I stared right back at him, without a flicker of doubt in my eyes.

He smiled then and talked of work, his friends, his family; how he dreamed of one day taking a man home to meet his parents.

He apologized for giving me the silent treatment, saying his anger was directed within. I laughed and apologized, because my waking-up-cranky was directed very fucking outward, to whoever's fucking there. He laughed, saying he had a pair of Oscar the Grouch socks that he'd gladly give me.

I kicked The Lone Ranger under the table.

Even back at work, he was the same. We set about our work at different tables, but every so often he looked over at me and smiled, which of course made me smile. I set my visual boards to print and my interview with the nightclub boys was done in a Powerpoint presentation. And with a final check of the time, I was done.

It was 3:08 AM.

We had 6 hours and 52 minutes to go.

6:52

I stood up, stretched and yawned. And yawned again. I was. So. Fucking. Tired.

"Hey," I said, walking up behind Cameron, squeezing his shoulder. "You nearly done?"

"No," he sighed. "The lighting is off on the boards, and I can't get the audio right on the video."

I rubbed my eyes and looked at his monitor. It looked pretty fucking perfect to me. "Cameron, it's fine."

"No, it's not," he said. "It needs to be perfect." He shook his head and scrubbed his hands over his face. "What the hell was I thinking? Bringing this new line in at the last minute? It's not going to be good enough."

I put my finger to his lips to shut him up. "Cameron, we're meeting with Lurex to offer them our brilliant best. That's why we're adding it at the last minute... because it was brilliant."

I replaced my fingers against his lips with my own and kissed him quick and hard.

"Now, show me what I can do to help."

He smiled but shook his head. "You get some sleep. I'll finish this off."

I objected, telling him we were in this together, and I wouldn't fucking sleep while he worked. He huffed, telling me it was his idea to add to our workload, so it should be him that has to do it.

"Don't fucking argue with me, Cameron," I said, rolling my tired eyes.

"Don't *you* fucking argue with *me*," he retorted. He was just as tired as me.

"Are you always this stubborn?" I asked.

"Yes," he answered. "Are *you* always this stubborn?"

"Yes."

He smiled, and I smiled. We both sighed. Then he pulled a chair up next to his own, and for the next three hours, we worked, side by side. We sat closely together, our knees touching and our hands sometimes rested on each other's thighs. We talked, we agreed, we disagreed, and we even fucking compromised. But when Cameron saved the file and sent it to print the photographic boards, we both leaned back in our chairs and sighed.

It had been sixty-one hours.

And now it was done. No going back, no changing anything. If it wasn't good enough now, it never would be.

"Come on," he groaned. "Let's take it all upstairs."

We both groaned when we stood, our aching bodies protested at the lack of sleep.

It was difficult to realize all our hard work comes down to eight visual boards and two video footage segments, each less than two minutes long.

We took it all to Cameron's office, dumping our laptops onto his desk then carefully setting the concept boards up. And for a quiet moment, neither of us spoke. We looked at our campaign, and then Cameron looked at me.

"Lucas," he said softly. "If we don't get this contract..." he looked back to the display boards, avoiding my eyes, "...it doesn't mean you're leaving, does it?"

"I hope not," I answered honestly. "I don't want to go."

He smiled, exhausted. Then stepped up to me, and his tired eyes closed. "I don't want you to go," he whispered and pressed his lips to mine. Just briefly, chastely, sweetly.

I smiled at him. He smirked, almost shyly. It was cute. "You want coffee?" he asked.

I nodded, "Mmm." And he walked slowly out the door toward the staff lunch room.

I pulled my phone from my pocket and checked the time.

It was six AM. Fuck. We were down to four hours.

4:00

I sat my ass down in the chair across from Cameron's desk and scrolled through my contacts. I knew it was early, but I also knew she'd be awake.

Her chipper greeting was met by my tired, dreary voice. "Morning, Rachel."

"What can I get for you? Do you need me to organize anything?" she asked, no nonsense, no small talk. Thank God.

"All, I need you to swing past my place. Grab me a suit, shirt, tie, shoes."

"No problem," she answered.

"Oh, and Rach?"

"Yes? Is there something else?"

"Yes." I grinned into the phone. "I need you to do me a favor."

CHAPTER TWELVE

I AM... OUT OF TIME

01:30

The next thing I knew, someone was shaking my leg and my fucking neck was killing me. My head lolled forward with a stabbing kink and my eyes opened.

Rachel.

"Come on," she said brightly. "It's time."

I fucking hate brightly.

I fucking hate cheery.

I noticed then, behind Rachel, was Simona, standing in front of a barely-awake Cameron.

He was in the chair next to me. We must have fallen asleep.

I jumped to my feet. "Shit. What time is it?"

Rachel laughed at me, so I sneered at her. I might have growled. Yes, it was rude. Yes, it was uncalled for.

I have issues about being woken up, okay? Don't act surprised. You saw how well it worked out when I was woken up by my phone yesterday at Cameron's.

Waking me up never worked out well, not for anyone involved. Just ask my Momma.

She spent my entire teenage years putting up with my hate-to-be-woken, rip-your-fucking-head-off ass.

"Don't try that shit with me, Lucas," Rachel stated with one hand on her hip. "It's 8:30. You have 90 minutes before your meeting."

I huffed. She was only tiny, this woman, but she sure kept me in line. "You sound like my Momma."

Rachel gave me one raised eyebrow, and Cameron chuckled. I glared at him and grumbled, "Don't you start."

Then he huffed out a laughed. Yeah, it was real funny, asshole.

I pointed my finger at him and opened my mouth to tell him he could stop fucking smiling, when someone cleared their throat. My head turned at the sound, and I winced and groaned at the shooting pain in my neck.

Mr. Fletcher.

"You boys look like Hell," he said. He looked at the girls, "Rachel, Simona, they need coffee, please. Strong, black. And some Tylenol for Lucas."

The girls nodded and disappeared, and I rubbed my neck. Mr. Fletcher smiled. "Falling asleep in these chairs is not good for your neck."

"Mmm," I moaned my agreement, trying to remember what happened -- why I fell asleep. "Cameron went to get coffee," I explained. "I sat down... and the next thing I know, I'm being woken up."

"You were asleep when I came back in," Cameron said. "I put the coffees on the desk, and sat down myself... I must have fallen asleep too." We both looked at his desk and there, along with laptops and papers, were two coffees, untouched.

"Mmm," Cameron's father hummed, his brows furrowed. "Have some fresh coffee, get showered and shaved. I'll organize some breakfast. I want to see you both after the Lurex appointment." And with that, he turned and walked out the door.

I stretched my neck a few times, working my head from side to side, and sighed loudly.

Cameron looked at me. "You okay?"

I looked at him and despite my none-too-cheery mood, I nodded. "You?"

He nodded, but before he could say another word, Simona came through the door, with a cup of steaming coffee. "Rachel has yours in your office," she told me.

I smiled, and remembering my manners, tipped my invisible hat to her. I looked at Cameron, wanting to say something, but not sure what, when Simona busied herself tidying, going on about what they need to do in just one hour. Seemingly oblivious to her talking, he looked at me and gave me a soft smile. I smiled back at him, without a word between us, in another one of those just-us moments.

Still smiling, for the first time ever, I gave Cameron a tip of my imaginary hat.

And fuck me, it made him blush.

Even though I was incredibly fucking tired, I grinned at his reaction and turned to walk out of his office into mine.

One hot coffee and two Tylenol later, I was standing in my shower. Both our offices had personal bathrooms. A little luxurious yes, but working for Fletcher Advertising, I wouldn't expect anything less.

I stood under the hot, streaming water, willing it to unknot my muscles and wake me the fuck up. And it worked, kind of. I felt better anyway. And after I shaved and brushed my teeth, I felt half alive.

Rachel had left my suit hanging behind the door, and

after I was dressed, minus shoes and socks, I remembered the little mission I'd sent Rachel on.

With bare feet, I padded out to my office. My office door was open, and I could hear Rachel and Simona talking from Cameron's office. But then I spied what I was looking for. There was a small shopping bag next to my shoes.

I peeked inside and grinned. Perfect.

Well, almost. I rearranged them just how I wanted them, and stuffed them back into the bag.

"Lucas?" Rachel's voice interrupted me. I looked up at her, and she was standing in the doorway. "There's some breakfast in Cameron's office."

"Thanks."

She nodded to the bag in my hand, speculatively. "Care to tell me what that's about? What I had to go to three different stores for?"

I shook my head and smiled. "No."

She smiled, despite her disappointment. Then leaning against the door, she said quietly, "If I told you I really, *really* wanted to know what went on between you two over the last sixty-odd hours, you wouldn't tell me, would you?"

I grinned and shook my head. "No."

She pursed her lips, rolled her eyes at me and sighed. With the bag in hand, I picked up my shoes and smiled at her as I walked barefooted across the hall into Cameron's office.

There was a platter of cut fruit and some croissants, juice and more coffee. "Eat up," Simona said. "We need you bright eyed and bushy tailed." Then she stopped, looking at my shoes in my hand to my bare feet. "Oh."

Cameron walked out of his en-suite bathroom, freshly showered and shaved, in tailored, charcoal suit pants and a crisp white shirt. He was pulling his sleeve cuff, doing up the button and didn't notice me at first.

When he looked up, his eyes went from Simona to me, to my shoes in my hands, to my bare feet and then to my eyes. He cocked his head, just a fraction and tried not to smile. "Forgetting something?"

I didn't answer him, instead I turned to Simona, and Rachel, who'd followed me in. "Can you girls give us a moment? Please, take the concept boards into the conference room and set up for us."

"Sure," Simona smiled with twinkling eyes and a suggestive look between us. She and Rachel collected the boards and laptop, and left us alone.

Cameron waited until the door clicked closed. "Lucas," he said lowly, a slight warning in his tone. His eyes flickered to the glass wall behind me. "What are you doing?"

I dropped my shoes onto the floor and held up the white shopping bag. "Jeez, Cameron. Give me some credit. I'm not gonna jump you at work, in the middle of the day."

Then I amended, "The middle of the night, yes. But not during the day."

He huffed at me, tried not to smile and failed. Then he looked at the bag in my hand again. I explained, "Oh, I got you something... well, I had Rachel get it, but it's from me."

He said nothing, but he was clearly surprised.

I dug my hand into the bag and pulled out his gift. A pair of socks.

A slow smile spreads across his face. "Superman?"

"And Clark Kent," I explained. "One of each." I held them up. "It took one pair of Superman socks and one pair of Clark and Lois socks, but I got a Clark and Superman pair."

He looked at me quizzically. So I explained, "Just like

you." I shrugged, and I was suddenly feeling a little nervous about this. I cleared my throat. "One who hides his true identity, and one who's kinda... *super.*"

He looked at me, right at me, his eyes bored into me, and we had ourselves another one of those moments. For a long second, we just stared at each other. The movement of someone walking past the glass wall broke our stare, and with a nervous chuckle, I handed over his socks.

"Thank you." He smiled shyly. "Lucas... it's very thoughtful." Then he looked at my bare feet. "What about your socks?"

"Oh," I said with a laughed. "I got some for me too!"

"Who'd you get?" he asked, his eyes shining and curious.

Grinning, I dipped my hand back into the bag and pulled out my socks dramatically.

"Han Solo and Chewbacca!"

"No way!" he gasped, excited.

I nodded and laughed, and sat down to put them on. "Come on," I urged him, with a pointed nod to the socks in his hand. "You have to wear them today, for this meeting."

He grinned and sat down in the seat behind his desk to unthread the laces on his shoes and take them off, then the socks he was wearing. I was just doing up the laces on my shoes when Cameron looked at me across his desk. "What happened to Lois?"

"Who?"

"Lois," he repeated. "You said one pair of socks was Clark and Lois Lane."

"Oh, *her*... she's in my trash can," I told him, nodding toward my office.

Cameron burst out laughing, just as his father opened the door. He grinned at the sight of his son laughing, just for a second. "Uh, boys? Ground floor reception just buzzed. The Lurex team are here."

Shit.

Cameron and I put on our jackets, and followed Mr. Fletcher to the conference room where our presentation was set up. We had just enough time to check everything was as it should be, the white-screen for the Powerpoint presentations was ready and our eight display concept boards were all turned around, awaiting the big reveal.

Mr. Fletcher smiled. "Good luck, boys," he said. "I'd love to sit in here with you," he said excitedly, "but don't want to put you off your game. So I'll have to settle for watching you two weave your magic from the CCTV screens in my office."

Oh, fuck. I'd forgotten he had full video link to the conference room.

"I'll have Simona and Rachel sit in and watch with me, if that's okay?" he asked. "I'm sure they'd love to see you two in your element."

Cameron smiled. "That's fine, Dad."

Mr. Fletcher smiled and walked through the doors that lead to his office, closing them behind him.

Cameron looked at me, and I at him. "Ready, Superman?" I asked.

He grinned and nodded. "Let's do this."

Sixty-five hours... I thought it was going to be an eternity. And suddenly, we were out of time. I took a deep breath, and the double doors opened.

CHAPTER THIRTEEN

I AM...IN AWE OF HIM

00:00

We were introduced to a team of three. A sharp-dressed woman, a short man who looked like Mole from Wind in the Willows, and a distinguished, older gentleman.

Carmen Renata, Stefan Vladimir, and the one and only Mr. Charles Makenna.

Pleasantries were exchanged, somewhat briefly, and Cameron hit the ground running. He just jumped right in. "Firstly, thank you for giving us this opportunity. We understand you're on a tight schedule, so I won't waste a minute of your time."

The three faces watched him.

He smiled. "Lurex needs Fletcher Advertising."

Well, that was an ice breaker.

I wondered if having his father watching would change his tactic, but it didn't. Cameron continued, so confidently. "Advertising in today's market is cutthroat. I don't need to tell you that. I also don't need to tell you Lurex sales have plateaued at eighty percent, and your closest competitor has grown six percent in the last two years.

"I don't need to tell you that.

"We're not here to tell you about *your* product. We're here to tell you about *our* product."

Cameron looked at me, giving me the floor.

I picked up right where he left off. "Fletcher Advertising isn't *just* about selling products. It's about providing solutions and concepts." I paused for effect.

The woman, Carmen Renata, spoke first. "Concepts? As in plural?"

"Yes," I replied confidently. "It's our job to ensure you stay ahead of the game against internet-enhanced global competition, fickle consumers and rapidly shrinking product lifecycles. By providing an advertising concept for different target markets, evolving as needed with continuous innovation to stay two steps ahead of your closest competitor. In today's economic climate, it's the only way to keep you ahead in the future long-term business game."

Mr. Vladimir wrinkled his nose when he spoke, making him look even more Mole-like. "And how do you propose to do that?"

I answered, "By providing a multi-faceted campaign targeting both gay and straight markets, as well as education and online strategies."

The three of them blinked, giving nothing away.

Cameron talked next. He talked, and they listened. I wondered briefly how proud his father would be of him, sitting just in the next room, watching his son right now.

Cameron's voice was quiet, but strong. They watched him and listened to him like they were here on *his* time, not the other way around. Hell, even I felt like I was here on his time.

He gave them figures, percentages and projection rates, then subtly brought their attention back to trends in consumerism. Which was my cue to elaborate on design concepts, focus marketing and selective advertising.

Then I turned six of the eight visual concept boards around to face them, showing the three visitors what we'd spent the last sixty five goddamn hours trying to perfect.

They looked good, even if I did say so myself. Six boards; three heterosexual, three homosexual. All exactly the same.

The picture of Ashley's delicate hand dipping below Ben's jeans matched the picture of Cameron's long fingers skimming the waist of mine. Both images were swathed in blue, both images were almost mirror-image perfect. Except one was of a man and a woman, and one was of two men.

The next pair of images were of torsos. The photograph with Ben's well muscled arms around his wife's tiny waist matched the photo of my arms around Cameron – when we were on the dance floor – my arms wrapped around him, my fingers spread wide against his skin. Both images were tinted pink to match the flash of the night club's lights.

And the third one was of feet. My favorite. They were in yellow hues, Ashley's dainty foot with painted toenails resting on Ben's. They were embracing, a position easily detected by the position of their feet. Just like the one of mine and Cameron's feet... his long, pale feet with perfect arches and perfect toes... with my feet in between them.

Mr. Makenna's stone expression didn't change. Carmen's eyebrows raised, as though she was silently surprised by the images, while Mr. Vladimir scrunched his nose. "There's no difference between them," he said, stating the fucking obvious.

He was either new to this, or he knew nothing about advertising. Possibly both. With more decorum than I had, Cameron smiled graciously. "That's because there is no difference between the couples, Mr. Vladimir. However one couple, on average, will purchase three times the amount of your product than the other." He stood confidently, walked to the window, clasped his hands behind his back. He wasn't even looking at them. He told them, statistically, gay men have more sex, and how the gay population was at its most sexually active between 18 and 35, and had on average, a national disposable income of millions, and that was a market that simply should not be ignored.

Mr. Makenna looked at Cameron, then at me. I could see he was thinking, but still he said nothing.

Taking the floor, I smiled at them. "This particular form of advertising can be used in women's magazines, men's magazines, online, billboards... the possibilities are endless." I looked at each of them in turn. "Television advertisements would be the same; interchanging the straight couple with the gay couple. Same positions, same lack of clothing, everything will be the same, except one couple is the same sex." I looked at Makenna. "I know you're thinking it's risky, it's provocative. But the point to this is to not discriminate between gay and straight, effectively ensuring at least eighty percent of the gay market will be inclined to purchase Lurex."

Ms. Renata and Mr. Vladimir both nodded, pensively.

I continued, "I have some video footage I'd like to share. It contains language not appropriate for delicate ears," I said, giving the lady a smile. "But if Ms. Renata approves, I think it's beneficial for the direction of this campaign."

Carmen Renata smiled at me. "Lucas, isn't it?"

"Yes, Ma'am," I confirmed my name.

"Lucas, it's fine. I don't mind the language," she said with a coy smile. "Thank you for the warning."

Yep, she liked me. I risked a quick glance at Cameron,

and I could tell he wanted to roll his eyes at me, but he didn't.

"This is... an impromptu focus group," I explained as I started the footage. The three of them watched as I appeared on the screen, calling out questions to my night club audience. But it was the responses of the men who answered, we were more interested in.

"A company like Lurex wouldn't have the balls to put gay men in an ad campaign."

"It's about time a rubber company got with the 21st century!"

My voice sounded onscreen, as I asked the crowd, "If you always used Lurex condoms, but another company brought out condoms for gay men, would you buy it?"

"Fuck yes!"

"Abso-fucking-lutely!"

I watched the three faces as they watched the footage as other questions were asked and answered. It only took a minute, but it was short, sharp and effective. When it ended, I said, "We've read all the group marketing Lurex has done over the years, but nothing quite as honest as that, wouldn't you say?"

Ms. Renata smiled thoughtfully, and Mr. Makenna tilted his head, contemplatively. But still he said nothing. Mr. Vladimir scrunched his nose, again. I was really starting to not like the man. He opened his mouth to say something, but Cameron spoke instead.

"The next line is aimed at education as well as marketing," his voice was so smooth. "Health care systems, providers, hospitals, community centres, youth centres, high schools, colleges."

He turned the two remaining boards to face them, and their reactions were immediate. The two boards were in black and white; one male, one female; both gaunt, drawn and obviously unwell. There was writing on each: 'Condoms cost less than a dollar. Not using one cost me everything' and the second one read, 'A condom is 80 cents. What will it cost you?'

Cameron told them, "Fletcher Advertising donates to a local respite centre that specializes in HIV care. I filmed this there," he said, starting the visual presentation. The footage of the two patients, Amy and James, started and our three guests watched in silence. It was confronting and so very fucking real. I got cold shivers watching it, hearing their short but tragic stories, how the mere cost of a condom, or more importantly, the lack-there-of, cost them so much.

Cameron stopped the footage, and the three Lurex executives stared at him. He frowned sadly and told them, "I think you get the point."

Then Cameron told them he knew it was the government's responsibility to provide education on health and safety. He knew it was risky to have a negative association with the product, but he also knew that Lurex donated in excess of one million dollars to research every year. A fact Lurex didn't advertise to the public.

A fact they *should* advertise.

Ms. Renata and Mr. Vladimir both nodded, and Mr. Makenna spoke for the first time.

"You're asking us to leave our current Advertising sector. Why should we leave Initiate Advertising? We've been with them for years."

"Yes, you have," Cameron agreed calmly. "And up until now, they've served you well. But they won't take you any further forward."

"And how will Fletcher Advertising do that exactly?"

"With all our clients," I intervened, "we have an initial

period where we use certain networking tools to gauge the public's reaction. If we don't believe the campaign is achieving as it should, we'll re-evaluate."

Ms. Renata looked a little surprised. "Networking tools?"

I nodded. "Depending on the product and the target age, we use different media forms to get real-time feedback. Given Lurex's target age bracket is 18-35, we'd focus on social networking sites."

Mr. Vladimir scrunches his nose. "*Facebook* and *twitter?*"

I looked him straight in the eye. "Amongst others, yes." Then looking to the other two Lurex members, I explained, "Using these sites gives us immediate and honest feedback. Not what a target market said six months ago, not what other focus groups were being paid to say, but what the consumer – the paying customer - thinks, right now."

I looked at Mr. Vladimir. "Using such sites shouldn't be dismissed. They're free, they reach a market of millions on a daily basis, they are easily accessible and they are real-time. Not six months ago, not last week, but," I tapped the table, "Right. Now."

Cameron said, "Fletcher Advertising has only had sixty five hours to research all Lurex has to offer, and in that time we've found your internet presence is severely lacking. We have specialized individuals here at Fletcher Advertising who can put you light years ahead of your competitors online. So," Cameron started to wrap up, "we've offered three components; the straight/gay couples, the 'what will it cost you?' educational line and incorporating these into our on-line strategy."

I finished off, "We would, of course, all need to set aside

more time so we can establish realistic short term and long term objectives to determine which strategy best suits you."

Charles Makenna looked at us both, and I could almost hear his mind ticking. "You've certainly done your homework."

I answered, "Of course we have. You shouldn't expect anything less from the company that will put your product name in every form of advertising there is."

"And you've done all this in sixty five hours?"

I nodded. He was impressed, I could tell. Then he asked, "What would you do differently if you had longer?"

I looked at Cameron. "Nothing," I said. Then I looked back at Mr. Makenna and told him outright, "I wouldn't do anything different."

Mr. Makenna was quiet for a moment, then he asked, "How do you know this will work?"

"Because we're the best at what we do," Cameron told him, a simple matter of fact. "And because you know it will. You run a multimillion dollar corporate business. You know what works. And you know, without a doubt, this will."

Mr. Vladimir did his best Wind-in-the-Willow's Mole yet. "Tell us again, why should we use you?"

I was one Texas-short fuse away from clearing the table and breaking his fucking nose, and Cameron must have sensed my mood, because he answered. "Mr. Vladimir, you're a numbers man, yes?"

Cameron's ability to read people was right on. The silly little man nodded proudly.

Cameron smiled. "You should use us because you don't want to explain to your shareholders why you turned down the opportunity to increase their profit by at *least* another five percent over the next twelve months."

It was brief, but I saw it. The corner of Mr. Makenna's

lip twisted in an upward direction. A smile. He turned to his peers. "Carmen, Stefan, if you don't mind, I'd like a moment," he very diplomatically asked them to leave.

The expression on their faces told me this didn't happen often. He stood with them, but waited until they'd left before he turned to us. He smiled, genuinely, this time. "Are you two always so confident?"

Cameron and I both answered at the same time. "Yes."

Mr. Makenna smirked. He was an older man, probably late fifties. He reminded me oddly of young Frank Sinatra, but with darker hair. Then, like he read my mind, he said, "Can I be frank?"

I almost laughed, but covered it with a cough. Cameron shot me a warning glance, before turning back to our guest. "Of course."

Mr. Makenna leaned against the large conference table. "It's a thorough campaign you've put on the table today, gentlemen. I have to admit I'm impressed."

I tried not to smile, while Cameron looked at him as though he expected nothing less.

Makenna continues, "It's got balls. It's gritty and it's honest. I like it. Pushing the gay concept is never easy, but I think you've done it well. I know you're both the best at what you do," he repeated our own words to us. Then he sighed. "You're both exceptional salesman... very confident..." his words trailed away, and I thought for a moment he was about to say no.

"...just *how* sure are you this gay aspect will work?"

"Mr. Makenna," I started, but Cameron cut me off.

"I know this will work, Mr. Makenna," he said, his eyes darted to the CCTV camera, then back to the man in front of us. "I know this will work, because I'm gay."

Holy fucking shit.

I looked at Mr. Makenna, trying to look as though Cameron's confession was nothing out of the ordinary. But my heart was thumping.... Jesus fucking Christ. Cameron's father, Mr. Fletcher was watching, listening. A fact Cameron was all too aware of, and he just came out.

Holy. Shit.

Holy. Fucking. Shit.

A slow smile spread across Makenna's face, a warm, almost thankful smile. Cameron's eyes looked over the man's shoulder, and I knew he was looking at the camera that feeds the CCTV. He was looking at his father.

Looking back at Makenna, Cameron said, "I know this target market. I know the product. And most importantly, I know advertising. This. Will. Work."

Under the circumstances, I did the only thing I could do. I stepped up beside Cameron. As much as I wanted to reassure him, hug him, touch him, I didn't. I just stood beside him, in a show of support, or a united front, if you will. He needed to know I'd stand beside him.

Makenna nodded, and I was still in fucking shock. My heart was thumping. I could only imagine how Cameron's must have been beating double time.

Then Mr. Makenna harrumphed with a smile and a shake of his head, like he couldn't believe this whole surreal experience. "I'll have my legal team be in touch for contracts," he said. He shook Cameron's hand, then mine, and walked out the door.

Holy fucking shit.

We did it.

We fucking did it.

I looked at the man beside me, and whispered, "Cameron...."

He looked at me, nodded and whispered back, "I know."

"Your dad...."

He nodded and swallowed. "I know."

Then the double doors behind us opened, the doors that joined the conference room to Mr. Fletcher's office. We turned to find Cameron's father standing there.

He didn't look at me. He was staring at his son.

I turned to look at Cameron. He was wide eyed and pale, and he was breathing way too hard.

"Cameron, look at me," I said, just to him. He did, and his eyes flickered to mine. He needed to know he didn't have to go through this on his own. "Do you want me to stay?"

He looked from me to his father and then to the floor between us. He shook his head slowly. "No."

"I'll just give you two a minute," I said as I turned to face Mr. Fletcher. His facial expression was one I'd never seen him wear. I couldn't be sure, but he looked like he was on the verge of tears.

I walked to the double doors Makenna just walked through and turned around to pull them closed behind me. But before the heavy wooden doors closed, I saw Mr. Fletcher cross the room quickly and wrap his arms around his son.

CHAPTER FOURTEEN

I AM... STARTING TO SEE THE BENEFITS OF CLOCKS THAT COUNT BACKWARDS

I WALKED BACK to my office in a daze.

We got the Lurex contract.

And Cameron just came out.

My head was spinning, and I think I needed to sit down. I slid into my desk chair, my head fell back and my eyes closed.

I heard my door open and Rachel's quiet voice. "Lucas?"

I opened my eyes. She was standing in the doorway with Simona, both wide eyed, shocked but smiling.

"You watched?" I asked.

They nodded.

"Cameron... Mr. Fletcher...." Rachel said, seemingly at a loss for words.

I waved the two girls in, and when the door closed behind them, I looked at Simona. "Will he be okay?" She knew I was referring to Cameron. I knew his father had hugged him, I saw it. But I was still worried for him. "If Cameron walks out of there upset, I swear... if his father makes it any more difficult for him...."

Simona shook her head. "No Lucas, he won't. I'm sure of it."

"Did you hear anything he said to him?" I asked.

Rachel shook her head. "We turned the monitor off when Mr. Fletcher hugged him. We left."

Simona asked me, "You knew he was gay?"

Nodding, I told her, "He told me."

She smiled. "I told him he could tell you."

I looked at Rachel and she explained, "I never knew for certain, he plays the straight guy role so well. But Simona told me on Friday night, when we left Cameron's place, that we should leave you two alone. And I knew then, for sure."

I looked at Simona. "When did he tell you?"

She nodded. "Long story, but suffice to say, one weekend when we were working together, I..." she grimaced, "...I hit on him, and he looked horrified. I kinda guessed."

I laughed. *Horrified.* I could just picture it.

"Ouch," Rachel said.

Simona nodded and laughed. "It wasn't as awkward as it could have been. Then I was the only one he could confide in," she added quietly.

It was quiet for a moment between the three of us. I still couldn't believe he just came out and said it with his father in our audience. I wondered what made him do it, what was the deciding factor, and I made a mental note to ask him when we had two minutes alone.

I smiled at the thought of being alone with him. I told him, twice, I wanted to see him outside of work. And I did. The word 'date' had even been mentioned....

"What's got you all smiling?" Rachel asked, looking at me.

I didn't even realize I was grinning. Fucking Hell, I felt

like a giddy schoolboy. "Nothing," I told them, though I think they could guess. "Come on, let's get this packed up," I suggested, looking at the piles of papers and files. Despite the serious lack of sleep, I felt kind of buzzed. I clapped my hands together, "Now the real work begins."

There was a quick rap on my door before it opened, and Mr. Fletcher's smiling face greeted me. "Lucas," he said, walking into the room. "You got Lurex!" he cried.

"We sure did!" I said with a grin. I kept packing up the files on my desk as I spoke to him. "Cameron just owned it. From the first word he spoke, he had them."

Mr. Fletcher looked toward the door, my eyes automatically followed his and saw Cameron standing there, listening. "You did your part, too," he said, slowly walking inside. "Of the three parts to the whole campaign, two were yours."

He smiled at me. He looked tired, exhausted, actually. I smiled back at him.

"Modesty really doesn't suit either of you," Mr. Fletcher said with a laugh. He walked up to us, positively glowing, and clapped one hand on each of our shoulders. "I know I said I wanted a meeting with you, but go home. Sleep. Both of you. I don't want to see either of you set foot in this office until 9 AM Wednesday."

"But," I started to object, looking at the paperwork on my desk.

"Are you arguing with me, Lucas?" Mr. Fletcher asked with a smile.

"No, sir."

He laughed, and all but pushed us out the door. I quickly grabbed my things, then realized I came to the office with Cameron. I turned and reminded him, "My keys, and my car are at your place."

He yawned. "No worries. I'll drive you there."

"Okay," I said, and he stifled another yawn. "Maybe I should drive," I suggested.

"Like hell," he mumbled. "You're not driving my car." And with that he turned and walked toward the elevators.

I looked at Mr. Fletcher, Rachel and Simona. They were all smiling at us. I rolled my eyes at them, and followed Cameron to the elevator. When we stepped inside and turned around, the three of them were watching us, grinning.

There were other people in the elevator with us, so we couldn't talk openly. Though I couldn't help but look at him and smile. He yawned twice more, and when we reached his car in the basement, he yawned again.

"Ugh," he groaned, shaking his head. "I'm so tired."

"Give me your keys," I said quietly. "Let me drive."

He pouted, but reluctantly handed over the keys to his car. Cameron fell into the passenger seat, his head leaning back on the headrest with his eyes closed. He looked tired, beautiful... peaceful.

"Cameron," I said softly, pulling the car out into traffic. "You okay?"

"Mm hm," he mumbled what I think was a yes. His head tilted, facing me and his eyes slowly opened. "Yeah."

"Big day, huh?"

He snorted. "Could say that." He shook his head. "I came out to my dad today," he said, like I didn't already know.

I smiled. "And there I was, thinking Lurex was the biggest thing on today's agenda."

He smiled, but he was quiet. His eyes were half closed, but he watched me as I drove.

"Your dad took the news okay?"

His eyes closed again, and he nodded. But he looked sad, almost.

My eyes darted from the road to his face. "You sure you're okay?"

He kept his eyes closed and nodded. "Just really tired."

I wasn't buying it. "Cameron?" I said, and his eyes opened. "Did he say something that upset you?"

"No," he answered. "He hugged me and told me he was so proud of me, that he loves me..." his quiet voice died away.

"That's good, right?" I asked, looking from his face to traffic and back to him.

He nodded, but then frowned. And I knew something was said between them, something that upset him, something that he didn't want to tell me. "Cameron, please, talk to me."

I could tell he was exhausted, and his eyes slowly closed again. "He took it too well," he said softly. "If I knew he was going to take it that well.... It makes me wonder just how much of my life I've wasted."

"Hey." I reached over and squeezed his hand. "None, not a minute. Don't think like that."

He shrugged, not convinced. "I'm so tired," he mumbled again.

He dozed while I had to concentrate on driving for a few minutes, and soon we were pulling up at his house. "Cameron?" I rubbed his thigh to wake him. "Come on, I'll get you inside."

He grumbled at me, but I helped him inside and I followed him as he trudged up the stairs. He literally fell onto his bed, fully dressed. I watched him for just a second before I decided to help him by pulling off his shoes, revealing one Clark Kent and one Superman sock. He chuckled and mumbled something about me and feet.

"I thought you were asleep," I said.

He smiled and tried to open his eyes. "Dunno why I'm so tired," he mumbled.

"Cameron, you've had about ten hours sleep in three days. And you came out today," I reminded him gently. "That's a helluva weight off your shoulders. It's gonna take a lot out of you."

He nodded and squinted his eyes as water beaded on his lashes. He covered his eyes with his hands, trying to hide his tears, but a quiet sob escaped him.

Oh, Cameron.

I sat beside him and peeled his hands from his face. "You don't have to hide from me," I told him softly, rubbing his cheek with my thumb. "You're allowed to cry, Cameron. You're exhausted, and it's been a stressful, emotional day."

Fresh tears fell, and he shook his head, betrayed by his own emotions. He cursed softly, "Fuck."

I leaned down and kissed his cheek. "It's okay, Cameron. You'll be okay."

He nodded and squeezed my hand. Without opening his eyes, he whispered, "Stay?"

Figuring he probably shouldn't be alone right now, I toed my shoes off and laid down beside him. And for the first time in my entire life, I fell asleep with a man, not exhausted from sex, not in a drunken haze.

But holding his hand.

I WAS SO COMFORTABLE. I was warm and cozy, in that blissful, dreamy place between asleep and awake. I felt like I should sleep longer, but somehow – a fucking miracle for me – I was strangely happy to be awake.

Until my comfy pillow moved.

And the blanket keeping me warm moved.

I grumbled at them sleepily, and then my pillow and blanket chuckled.

I looked up, trying to make sense of my thoughts, and I saw him.

Cameron.

My pillow and blanket was Cameron; a half asleep, chuckling Cameron. I groaned and let my head fall back on his chest, his arms tightened around me. "I wondered why my pillow moved."

He chuckled again, and I could hear the sound resonate in my ear. Rolling off him, I stretched out my legs. We were both still fully dressed in our suit pants and shirts and I was lying right next to him, our sides were still touching. I propped my head up on my bent arm.

"You feel okay?"

He nodded and smiled shyly. "Thanks for staying. And I'm sorry I got emotional before."

"Cameron," I said, my voice and my stare were serious. "Don't apologize. You, my dear man, are an out and proud gay man. Keep your fucking chin up, okay?"

He inhaled sharply and his eyes shone. "I don't have to hide anymore, do I?" he asked softly, a statement more than a question.

I shook my head and smiled at him, and we had another one of those moments where we just stared at each other. You'd think I'd be used to them. I'd had so many with him, but they still made my heart thump weirdly. Then he reached up and glided his long fingers along my jaw, sending shivers down my spine.

"Lucas," he breathed my name, then pulled me in so he could kiss me.

I opened my mouth for him. It was a slow, sleepy, languid kiss, gentle lips and unhurried tongues. His eyes were closed, and he was so into this kiss. His hand kept hold of my jaw while his other arm wrapped around my back.

Not breaking the kiss, I leaned over him, so I was lying on top. I rested my weight on my elbows and my hands cupped his face. He groaned when I settled my hips against his, our cocks touching through the fabric of our pants.

He tilted his head and opened his mouth wider, as he ran his hands over my back. He pulled my shirt out of my suit pants, and then I could feel his hands on my skin, over my back, my shoulders. He gripped me. His fingers tried to find purchase, but my shirt must have got in the way.

Because then he was trying to undo the buttons, his mouth kissed down my jaw, and he growled in frustration. I could feel the urgency in how his hands trembled.

I pulled his hands from my shirt front and pinned them at his sides. His eyes widened, and I smiled. "Slow, Cameron. Slow," I said, kissing down his neck. "I said I wanted to take my time with you."

He whimpered, so I nipped at his Adam's apple. I could feel his cock twitch. I let go of his hands and got to my knees, one each side of his hips. I fingered the buttons on his shirt, popping each one slowly, teasingly. His eyes were dark, his lips were red and swollen, but he smirked. "You're gonna kill me," he said, his voice thick with desire.

I pulled his shirt open and leaned down to peck his lips. "Many deaths," I whispered, my nose touching his. "Many, many deaths."

He chuckled, and I took my time undressing him. I exposed every inch of his skin like a gift, just for me. I pressed my lips to his chest, his stomach, his hip, his thigh. Kneeling between his legs, I lifted his feet and peeled off his socks. I bade Superman and Clark Kent adieu, making Cameron shake his head at me and laugh. Still holding one of his feet, I bit the perfect arch of his foot, playfully gnashing my teeth along his skin. He grinned, but he was breathing harder, his eyes were darker.

I didn't take near the care for my own clothes, ripping them off quickly and tossing them to the floor. He was naked before me, and when I was naked between his legs, I leaned over him once more. "Cameron, tell me now if you don't want this..."

Without a word, he leaned over to his bedside table, opening the drawer and pulling out foil packets and a bottle of lube. But I needed to hear him say it. "Tell me."

His voice was gruff and quiet. "I want you." His hands cupped my jaw, my neck. "I want you to have me, take me... fuck me."

A ripple of desire rattled me, and I smashed my mouth to his. I slid my body against his, my tongue against his. The heat and steel of his cock rubbed against mine until I pulled back from him so I could open the foil square packet and rolled the condom onto my cock. I looked at him, without any more words, without any more doubts.

And then he did it - that beautiful surrender. He spread his legs for me.

Vulnerable, open and giving, and I devoured him. I kissed, licked and sucked on his neck, his nipples, his navel. I licked his cock, then sucked his balls into my mouth. He was squirming, groaning and pleading at my touch, and he didn't hear the click of the lube bottle. When I took his swollen head into my mouth, he bucked and moaned, and I slipped my finger into his ass.

He gasped and writhed, and I sucked and consumed. I pumped his shaft and pulled his sac and probed his ass. He gripped the sheets at his sides and arched his back, and as his cock slipped into my throat, I slipped a second finger into him.

He cried out and his cock swelled in my mouth making me hum and moan around him. When I slipped a third finger into his willing ass, curling my fingers around to his prostate, he bucked and fucked my mouth. With a final cry, Cameron flexed rigid, and his cock erupted, surging hot come down my throat. I swallowed what he gave me.

Violent shudders ripped through him, and I fell forward on my hands. While he was still riding his orgasm high, I pressed my aching cock into his ready hole. His eyes flew open, only to slowly close as his head pushed back into the pillows, his neck corded and strained. His cock was jerking, pulsing, leaking.

I pushed every inch of me into him, and he took it, all of me. My God, this was Cameron. I was fucking Cameron. I kissed him, letting him taste himself on my tongue, fucking his mouth while I fucked his ass.

But it was slow, sensual, we were rocking and sliding. It was so fucking good. He pulled his mouth from mine and groaned in my ear. "I've imagined this," he whispered.

I pulled back, resting on my forearms, so I could see his face. My hips never stopped pumping into him, slowly, deeply.

"I've dreamed of this," he told me, moaning and arching with every thrust.

"Is it what you imagined, Cameron?" I asked in his ear. I took his earlobe between my teeth and licked it. "Is it?"

"Better." He gasped, clawing at my skin with his blunt nails. "Fuck, so good."

Reaching down, I hitched one of his legs up, forcing my cock deeper inside him.

"Ah," he cried and bucked, and I could feel his solid cock swell between us.

"You're still hard," I grunted into his neck. I was leaning on one arm, holding his leg with the other, so I told him, "Pump your cock for me."

So he did. He slid his hand between us and worked his hand up and down, pumping himself as I continued to fuck him. I wasn't going to be able to hold off much longer; he was too tight, too hot and I was too hard, too close.

"Again," he rasped. "My God, again. Fuck. Gonna come again."

And that was it. My self-control snapped. "Yessss," I hissed, hot in his ear, thrusting harder. "I wanna feel you come when I'm buried inside you."

His hand pumped faster, and I thrust harder. I was right there, so close. I thrust hard, filling him, once, twice, three times. I kissed him, long and deep, as he came again.

I swallowed his cries as his cock spilled, hot and thick between us while his tight ass clamped around my shaft. I fucked him, hard, hard, hard, and the room spun, and there was no sound as my cock emptied into the condom.

As I floated back into my body, I was aware of feeling hot, sweaty and sticky and feeling really, really fucking good. I was aware of feather light fingers tracing patterns on my back and kisses in my hair.

I didn't want to pull out of him. I could have stayed inside him forever. But I had to, and reluctantly I did. I kept my hold on him, and he kept his arms around me like neither of us wanted it to end.

We lay like that until our breathing slowed. "Shower?" I asked.

"Sure," he answered. "I'll get you a fresh towel."

I leaned up on his chest and smiled. "You're coming in with me," I told him. "I'm nowhere near done with you yet."

He laughed, and I got up off him and gently pulled him to his feet. I asked him if he was okay, and he promised he was. "Actually, I'm better than okay," he amended. "So much better than okay."

In the shower, I soaped him up and washed him down, taking extra care of his ass. I washed his hair, and kissed his lips and when we were done, I dried him off.

I stepped into his walk-in-wardrobe and helped myself to clothes. We were similar height and build, so his jeans and shirt fit me just fine. "You don't mind, do you?" I asked with a smirk, doing up the jeans.

He watched me, with a towel around his waist, and shook his head. "Not at all."

I grinned back. "Stay here, in your room," I told him. "We'll lie in bed and watch some TV," I said, nodding pointedly at the flat screen on the wall. "I'll just grab us some water. Want something to eat?"

He shook his head no, still smiling. "Maybe later."

When I got downstairs, the first thing I noticed was it was getting dark outside, and I had no idea what the time was. The second thing I noticed was that damn, fucking countdown clock. It was flashing zeros at me.

And it gave me a fucking great idea.

I grabbed two bottles of water and the countdown clock. When I got back upstairs, I detoured into the bathroom to collect the second bag of Lurex goodies.

Grinning like a fool, I walked back into Cameron's bedroom. He was lying on his bed, dressed in jeans and a tee, propped up on pillows with his phone in his hand. "Just got a text from Mom," he said quietly, without looking up.

"She wants me to call her when I 'wake up'." He looked hesitant.

"Cameron, you came out today," I reminded him gently. "She was going to want to speak to you."

He nodded and sighed. "Yeah, I know. I just want some time to get my own head around it before reality kicks in," he said. "I'm not hiding."

I nodded. "I know. Take all the time in the world. They're going to want to talk about it and you need to be ready."

He smiled, relieved. Then he looked at what I was holding. "What are you doing?"

I grinned at him. I dropped the bottles of water onto the bed and dropped the Lurex bag onto the floor so I could put the countdown clock on his dresser.

Plugging it in, I grinned and ask him, "What time is it?"

He looked at his phone, "Um, six fifteen?" He really had no idea what I was doing.

I quickly did the math and set the clock.

38:45

"That, my dear man, is how much time we have before we have to go back to work on Wednesday morning."

He looked at me, clearly confused.

I picked up the brown paper bag and upended the Lurex goodies onto his bed. The nude colored dildo, silver prostate wand and an array of condoms and lube sample packets spilled onto the sheets. "And these, my dear man, are how we shall spend it."

A slow smile spread across his face, and I crawled up onto the bed, kissing him softly on the lips.

Then I chuckled and rubbed my chin, like I was thinking. "You know, if we brought up the white board, we could add your precious time increments for each product," I said, looking at the assortment of Lurex products we had to play with. "You know, so we can track our product/time ratios."

He gasped, like I offended him, but he was smiling. He looked at the clock, then at the Lurex products and then at me. He grabbed my shirt and pulled my face an inch from his. His hazel eyes blazed and he licked his lips. "Shut the fuck up, Hensley. You're wasting time."

CHAPTER FIFTEEN

I AM...FALLING FOR HIM

38:45

Cameron kissed me. Fuck, how he kissed me... so sure, so demanding. His tongue was so commanding in my mouth, his hands were strong and in charge of my body.

He pulled his mouth away, and we both gasped for breath.

"God," he groaned, kissing down my neck. "How could I want more? You've already made me come twice...."

"Is that a challenge?" I asked, breathily. "Because, my dear man, I can do better than just two."

His eyes flashed, and he was about to say something, but then my phone buzzed and Proud Mary by Creedence blared from my suit pants still on the floor.

Cameron gave me one raised eyebrow and a smirk, and I poked him in the ribs, telling him, "It's my Momma's ringtone."

He laughed and rolled off me, and I rolled off the bed to collect my phone. "I better take this," I told him.

He smiled. "I'll organize some food. Come down when you're done."

I nodded and answered my phone. "Hey, Momma!"

38:32

Downstairs, I found Cameron busy in the kitchen chopping greens and other vegetables. He smiled at me. "Everything okay back home?"

I nodded. "Yeah. I just got in trouble for not calling her last night. I usually give her a call on Sunday nights and clean forgot last night." I sat down at the island bench. "She was about to start calling hospitals and police stations," I said with a laugh and rolled my eyes.

Cameron looked up at me and grinned. When he turned his back to me, to heat the wok, I stole a handful of carrot strips. He looked back at me. "Did you pick off the chopping board?"

I shook my head and smiled, trying to swallow the evidence and subsequently started to choke.

And the bastard smirked. "Serves you right," he said. In something close to sympathy, he handed me a beer.

"Yeah, thanks," I barked out between coughing fits.

He chuckled, and I tried to dislodge the carrot with a mouthful of beer. He laughed when it only made me cough more and my eyes water, and I called him a handful of names.

He smiled, adding a bit of this and dash of that from different bottles out of the pantry and ten minutes later, we were eating stir-fry.

It was really good. In all fairness, it was better than mine.

Not that I'd ever tell him that.

37:48

We talked through dinner. It was easy, without effort. He was really quite funny. He told me stories of his youth, when he tried to like girls and when he realized, without doubt, he was gay.

"When did you come out?" he asked.

"I was fifteen. My Momma told me I was gay."

"Your *Momma* told you?" he asked incredulously. He was trying not to smile.

"We'd been watching the men's diving on TV," I explained, and Cameron nodded in understanding. "She told me to close my mouth because I was drooling."

He chuckled. "Your Momma sounds like one hell of a woman."

I rolled my eyes. "Oh, you have no idea."

He picked at the label on his beer. "So, you've always been open about who you are? Even in high school and college?"

I nodded. "Yep."

He flinched a little, as though his coming out at twenty-six years of age isn't good enough – or that I made it sound easy. "Cameron, high school for me was a living, fucking Hell. I was picked on, bullied, beaten up... you name it, I went through it."

He looked at me with wide eyes. "I'm sorry," he said.

"What for?" I asked. "No, I didn't have it easy, but every time they called me names, every time they shoved me into the lockers, it only made me stronger, more determined."

We were quiet for a moment. I picked up our plates off the table. "It's never easy at any age," I said, walking to the kitchen.

He followed me. "You know, that's what made me do it."

I looked at him, questioningly.

"That's what made me say it... to Makenna... to come out like that," he explained.

I stopped my cleaning up and look at him, giving him my full attention.

"Makenna was what, fifty? Maybe fifty-five years old?"

I nodded. "Yeah, about that."

"And he had to ask his staff to leave so he could speak freely," Cameron said. "I didn't want to be like him. It just hit me, I was twenty-six. Every day I didn't do it, was another day I'd lost. I didn't want to be some old guy still too scared to fucking live, ya know?"

I nodded. "I know."

"And it was like a now or never moment," he said. "The words... I just said them. My heart was beating so hard. I thought I was going to pass out."

I smiled at him. "You were fucking awesome," I told him, making him blush.

Then his phone beeped with another message. "Ugh," he groaned. "It's Dad."

He read the message aloud. *For God's sake, please call your mother!*

I chuckled at him. "I'll tidy up. Put your dad out of misery, and go call your mom."

Ten minutes later, I was done. The kitchen was tidy, and I walked toward the sound of Cameron's voice. "Tomorrow afternoon Mom, come around tomorrow. I just need some time... yes, I will... no, Mom, I'll call Ben... mm hmm," he nodded. Then his eyes darted to mine, and he spoke into the phone, "Well, actually, he's still here."

There was a brief silence, then he said to me, "Mom said 'hello'."

I grinned. "Hello, Mrs. Fletcher," I said, loud enough for her to hear.

Cameron held the phone out from his ear, and I could

hear a shrill squeal. Cameron mumbled into the phone, "Yeah, thanks Mom. That's not embarrassing at all."

I laughed and knelt on the sofa beside him. Slowly, I swung my leg over so I was straddling him. His eyes went wide, and his head fell back so he was looking up at me.

"Ah, Mom, I have to go...."

I leaned down and licked his jaw. He hummed.

"...yeah, tomorrow...."

I sucked his earlobe between my lips. He shuddered.

"...make it late... after lunch...."

I scraped my teeth over his neck and bit at his skin. He gasped.

"...ah, okay... mmm... sure... bye, Mom."

He threw his phone onto the lounge and groaned. "You don't play fair."

"I play to win," I said with a chuckle, and trailed my lips up his jaw to his mouth. "We've wasted enough time. That countdown clock is awfully lonesome upstairs."

36:08

I knelt on his bed and beckoned him over, slowly pulling him onto the bed with me. I laid back, dragging him with me, so he was on top. He moaned, and gooseflesh crawled over my skin at the sound.

I lifted his shirt off, baring his beautiful chest. He soon discarded mine, and his wandering hands roamed every inch of my skin.

I could feel the bulge and the heat of his hard-on. And he could feel exactly how much he was turning me on.

But he didn't move to take my jeans off.

Not yet, anyway.

35:28

He moaned, throwing his head back.

"Mmm, there it is," I moaned. "Does it feel good, baby?"

He moaned his assent. "Fuckyessss."

I was kneeling between his thighs, his knees were raised. One of his hands pumped his swollen cock, and his other hand eased the prostate wand in and out of his well-lubed ass.

I was watching him as he did it, encouraging him, while I stroked myself. He was so fucking beautiful. The sheen of sweat that covered his long, pale body; how his muscles bunched and contracted under his skin, his abs and thighs flex as his orgasm neared. His face... ohmygod, his face....

His eyes were closed, his jaw was tight, his mouth was open. "Fuck, fuck, oh fuck," he was moaning.

"Open your eyes, baby," I coaxed him. "Watch what you do to me."

His eyes opened, and he looked at my face then his eyes trailed down to my cock. I fisted myself harder, faster.

He cried out, "Oh, fuck Luc yes, please, please..." His back arched, and he squeezed his cock, sending cum surging across his stomach. His orgasm summoned my own, pulled from inside my bones, pleasure so pure spurt hot and thick across his skin.

34:16

"You can't have them," I said again. "They're mine!"

He laughed. "Pleeeeeeease," he begged and batted his eyelashes.

"Not even the dazzling powers of the almighty Cameron Fletcher will make me give in," I warned him with a laugh. "The Han Solo and Chewbacca socks are mine."

He bounced up on his knees and straddled me, pinning my arms at my sides.

Laughing and smiling beautifully, he demanded, "Name your price, Hensley."

32:04

"Mmmm," I moaned. "Right there."

"Feel good?" he whispered into the back of my neck.

"Oh yes, so good," I mumbled, my face pressed into his pillows. I was lying face down, and he was straddling me. I was naked, he was naked and digging his oh-so talented fingers into my shoulders.

I think he may have gone a little overboard with the Lurex Play Massage Oil, because we were covered in it.

It was slippery and slick, then for some reason only known to Cameron, he thought it would be funny to try and tickle me.

Except I bucked when he dug into my ribs, and he slid clear off the bed.

I laughed so hard I had to pee.

It costs me my Star Wars socks.

31:46

"Oh, holy shit!" Cameron cried. "They really do glow in the dark!"

I returned to the bed after flipping the light switch and knelt back on the bed. "I told you!" I shuffled up to him, both of us on our knees, our illuminated cocks protruding between us.

Then he laughed. "They look like lightsabres."

Oh, dear God.

I couldn't help but laugh. "If you start making lightsabre noises, I'll take back my socks."

He snorted. "Hmmmm, look at that. My lightsabre's longer than yours..."

I gasped, deeply offended and just slightly amused. "Mine's thicker," I hissed at him, pushing him backward on the bed. I wrapped my hand around his long, green *lightsabre*. "How funny will it be with my lightsabre buried in your ass?"

He groaned, thrusting his hips up at me, daring me, urging me.

Fifteen minutes later, he was on all fours, writhing, and my cock was pulsing deep in his ass. I could see the illuminated green of my dick disappear in his hole, sliding in and out, faster, deeper. He threw his head back and groaned long and low.

I leaned over him and spoke rough in his ear. "How do you like it now? Long enough, thick enough?"

And he reared up onto his knees and cried out a guttural growl as he came into his glow-in-the-dark condom. His ass clenched my cock, and his body convulsed as I fucked him hard until I came.

31:16

Exhausted and thoroughly fucking sated, I found a washcloth, wet it with warm water and took care of Cameron. He was almost asleep, face down, so I carefully cleaned him.

When I crawled into bed beside him, he settled his head on my chest. I wrapped my arms around him, and he snuggled into me, already asleep.

I brushed his hair back, kissing the top of his head.

I fell asleep, very satisfied.

And very happy.

23:34

I woke up slowly, and funnily enough, in a pretty good mood. It was bright, I was so damn comfortable and I felt as though I'd slept for a week.

But I woke up alone.

I stretched out and eventually sat up, looking around Cameron's room at the mess we'd made. There were foil packets everywhere, some open, some not, the sheets were a mess, there were towels on the dresser and clothes on the floor.

It looked like two guys just spent hours in here fucking.

Oh, wait.

We did.

I smiled.

I got up and put on my jeans – well, actually they were Cameron's jeans – and headed downstairs. I could hear him in the kitchen, and I smiled when I saw him.

He was just wearing jeans and a tee-shirt, he was un-showered and unshaven, cooking breakfast. "Oh, hey," he said with half a smile. "I was just making something to eat. I woke up starving."

I chuckled. "I'm not surprised," I said with a smile. "We burned some energy last night."

"Well, you woke up in a good mood," he said. He was so fucking smug.

I looked him up and down, from his smug smile to his oh-sweet-Jesus bare feet. I looked back up to his face. "Well, I can't take all the credit."

He grinned and blushed, going back to his frypan. "Do you like eggs and bacon?"

"Does it come with coffee?"

He grinned. "Can you make it?"

I rolled my eyes at him. What kind of stupid question was that?

22:12

"Here, grab the corner," he instructed.

I folded the corner of the sheet and lifting the mattress, tucked it in. "Don't know why we're bothering to remake the bed? We're only gonna mess it up again."

He chuckled. "It was your idea!"

"Yeah well, the sheets were a mess," I told him. "But look on the bright side... now we get to mess them up again!"

I picked up the dildo and flopped down onto my back on the freshly-made bed. "You know, we haven't used this yet."

Cameron bit his lip, then looked at the clock. He groaned, "Mmmm, Mom and Dad will be here in a few hours."

"A few hours, huh?" I pondered out loud. Plenty of time.

"I'm sorry," Cameron apologized.

"What for?"

"Spending time with my parents is probably not how you envisioned spending the last twenty hours," he said.

I waved the dildo at him. "Rest assured it's not... I mean your dad's a good looking man, but he's too old for me..." I said, joking with him.

Cameron gasped, his mouth falling open. I laughed at his expression, and he surprised me by launching himself at me, pushing me into the mattress and pinning my hands down at the sides of my head. He was deceptively strong and fast. He grinned, looking down at me with daring in his eyes. "Is that so?"

I smiled and nodded. "Yeah, and he's straight too... really not my type at all."

He laughed and still holding my arms down, he sat on my stomach. I eyed his crotch; the fly of his jeans was right in front of me. He thrust his hips forward. "See something you like?" he asked, waving his denim clad cock in my face. "Looking a little hungry there, Lucas," he teased.

Playful Cameron was a dangerous and very fucking sexy Cameron.

I groaned. "Mmm, always. Now I know what you taste like," I teased him back. "I could eat your cock all day."

"Fuck," he moaned, and I chuckled.

He couldn't beat me at this game.

He was still sitting on me, but he let go of my arms so I reached up and grabbed his hips.

Pushing him down, I sat up, so he was straddling me. His face was close to mine, and I looked right in his eyes and told him, "A few hours is plenty of time."

He grinned. "Plenty of time for what?"

I licked my lips and whispered gruffly, "Plenty of time to fuck your face with my cock, then fuck your ass with the dildo until you beg me to let you come. Plenty of time to suck you, lick you, rim you and then, *then* fuck you again."

His breath hitched, and his eyes rolled back.

I smirked at him. "But before any of that, *you* are gonna fuck me."

His eyes widened, and I ran my hands through his hair, pulling his face closer to mine. "I want your dick in my ass. I want to know what it's like to have you inside me."

His eyes rolled closed, and he shuddered. I pecked his lips, and he reacted by kissing me hard, brutally crushing his mouth on mine. Deep and slow, real and right. He held my face, my neck, his fingers threaded through my hair, and I melted. I fucking melted.

My bones turned to warm jello, and I fell into him. He pushed my body down, aligning me properly and settled his weight on me. It felt fucking divine.

And right.

It never felt so right.

He kissed me deeper, longer, somehow softer. He was so in charge of this kiss. And I knew I would give myself to him. I knew it. I wanted it.

I'd bottomed a few times and enjoyed it. I mean, with the right partner it was fucking great.

But this was different....

I didn't just *want* to bottom with him. I *needed* it. There was a desire in my belly, warm and achy, that needed Cameron to fuck me. A craving at the base of my spine I knew would only be sated when he was inside me.

And that was new. I'd never felt that before.

My mind spun in circles and he was still kissing me, our mouths were open wide, and his tongue was sliding slowly against mine. My hands pressed the small of his back as he pressed me into the mattress. And it hit me, like a ton of fucking bricks, my desire to give myself to him, to let him fuck me, wasn't a physical desire. It wasn't physical at all.

It was emotional.

I was falling for him.

He felt me freeze underneath him, and he pulled his mouth from mine. His eyes shimmered with lust and light, and I thought he might see my realization staring back at him.

I knew he felt the same. He admitted to wanting me for months, that I was all he could think about....

"Luc, you okay?"

I could feel my eyes widen with understanding. I was falling for him, like he was falling for me. I nodded. I am okay. "Yeah," I tried to say, but my voice was just a whisper.

"Are you sure you want me to..."

I nodded. I've never been more sure of anything. "Cameron, I'm sure."

21:48

Oh, fuck.

It hurts. Hurts so good. Fuck.

He was sucking on the head of my cock, licking with his swirling tongue, and pumping my shaft. And he had his fingers in my ass, prepping me, stretching me.

Fuck.

Fuck.

"Cameron, please," I begged him. "I'm ready. I need you, Cam... inside me... when I come..."

I wasn't making sense, but my mind was splintered, and my body was on fire. My skin was burning painlessly, my bones were heated through. Then he was inching inside me, his long, slick shaft, stretching me, spearing me, slowly, surely.

And it wasn't enough.

I lifted my hips and wrapped my legs around his back, and he fell forward on his hands, his cock pushing deeper inside me.

"Oh, fuck," he breathed. "Oh, God."

Leaning on his elbows, he pushed my hair back. His hands cradled my face, and he kissed me, softly, tenderly. His tongue swept my mouth, tenderly, reverently. He was fully inside me, every fucking inch was buried inside me; I could feel the square of his hips on my ass.

He didn't thrust his hips. He rocked, gently rolling his hips, pressing deeper into me each time as his lips and his tongue stayed infused to mine.

And we were not fucking.

I think... I think....

...we were making love....

"Oh, Cam," I gasped.

I could feel his body tremble. He was trying to stave off his orgasm. "It's too much," he whispered against my lips. "Fuck, Luc."

Leaning on one elbow, he slipped his other hand between us. He gripped my cock, sliding and twisting his hand up my shaft and over the head.

And he started to mumble in my ear. "So hard... fuck,

fuck, so tight... so hot... my cock.... so far inside you... never dreamed... it could be this good...."

His breath was hot and wet against my skin and in my ear. And I was right fucking there, so close, so close, if he'd just push into me harder, I'd come. I couldn't take any more. I gripped his shoulders and tightened my legs around him. "Oh God, Cameron. Ohmygod, fuck me, please. Fuck me, fuck me."

He was quick to lean up on one hand, changing the angle of his cock buried in me, and he thrust hard. He gripped my engorged dick harder, fisting me so fucking hard, I arched into him as I erupted between us.

I think I screamed.

I think I died a beautiful death.

I was aware of only him. Only Cameron. He bucked and shuddered, and bucked again. His whole body trembled and with a keening growl, he came. I could feel the surge and swell of his cock in my ass as he filled and filled and filled the condom.

He fell on top of me, still twitching inside me, kissing every part of my neck he could reach. He pulled out of me, even though I didn't want him to. I wanted him to stay on me, in me, all around me. I closed my eyes for just a moment, and then he was waking me, telling me the bath was ready.

20:56

The water was hot and up to our necks. He sat facing me, his legs on the outside of mine. The bath was deep and big, it was an old cast iron original. It was divine.

My head lolled back against the tiles, my eyes were closed, my body spent.

It was a tranquil silence between us, and it gave me time to think.

My stark realization, earlier, that I was falling for this man, was playing around in my head. It was an idea I could possibly get used to. It was a new concept for me, all in all, and I couldn't help but wonder what it was about him that had captured me.

Then I felt it.

His foot. On my chest.

I opened my eyes, and his long, pale, wet, slightly pruned foot was a few inches from my face. His eyes were closed and he was grinning. He was teasing me because he knew I had a thing for feet... he was toying with me.

So I grabbed his foot and bit it. Gently, I nipped at the arch and the ball of his foot. He was watching me now, still grinning and he lifted his other foot, offering it to me as well.

So I bit it too. Then I kissed it and sucked his toe between my lips. He smiled, and his eyes were fixed on my face. I held his feet near my face, rubbing it along my cheek, and stared back at him.

And neither one of us said a word.

20:13

It was the first time we'd ventured outside in God only knew how long. We'd arrived at a deli that Cameron apparently frequented, just two blocks away. I held the door for him, and as he walked inside, my hand found the small of his back.

And he froze.

I dropped my hand, and we walked to the counter. "I'm sorry," he said quickly. "I'm sorry. It's habit... I'm not used to it."

I smiled at him, forgetting how new he was to this. "Sorry, I didn't think..."

"No, it's okay," he said. Then he looked at me. "It is okay, isn't it?"

I nodded my head and he exhaled. We stood at the counter waiting to be served, and he rocked back and forth on his heels. I looked at him, and he grinned.

When the small lady behind the counter asked us what we'd like, Cameron leaned forward, putting his hand on my waist, and asked me which salad I'd like. I grinned at him. He was touching a man in public for the very first time. It was gentle and barely there, but to anyone looking, they'd know it was a public display of affection. "You choose," I said in his ear.

He ordered an array of antipasto and salads, and I smiled at him as I handed over the cash to pay. He was positively glowing. When I looked at him, he whispered, "Thank you."

I picked up lunch and told him, "You're very welcome."

And he grinned the entire way home.

CHAPTER SIXTEEN

I AM...THE GIVER OF SWAGGER

18:42

"I thought you said you were going?" he asked, grinning. He was sitting on a dining chair, and I was sitting on him, straddling him. We didn't get too far after lunch.

"I am," I said, kissing down his neck. "I just want to make out with you a little more..." I mumbled into his skin. "You're rather addictive."

He chuckled as his hands skimmed my sides. "Is that so?"

I looked into his eyes, and he stared at me. His smile faded, and we had another one of those moments; serious and something unsaid passed between us. I nodded. "Yes."

I wasn't entirely sure what I answered yes to - was he addictive; did I want more; did he make my heart thump funny – but I kissed him. Deeply.

His hands braced my face, and our tongues met. He sat up taller as though he was trying to get deeper in my mouth.

And the doorbell rang.

"Shit," he cursed. He looked wide eyed at me, then he

looked at his watch. "That's my parents. I didn't realize the time."

Fuck. Well, this could be awkward.

"I'm sorry," he apologized again.

"S'alright, Cameron. And stop apologizing," I told him again, getting off his lap. "Go and let them in, I'll tidy up this mess," I said, waving my hand at the plates still on the table.

I started picking up plates and I heard him greet his mother, and turned in time to see her almost tackle-hug him into the hall. I smiled and walked into the kitchen.

I'd barely got the plates in the sink, in fact I was still holding one of them, when Mrs. Fletcher walked through to the kitchen. Her eyes beamed, she turned from me to her son and back again, then she tackle-hugged me.

Luckily, Mr. Fletcher grabbed the plate I was holding. Cameron mumbled, "Oh, for the love of God, Mom, please..."

She whispered, "Thank you," in my ear before Cameron dragged her off me, leading her to the back patio. He mouthed, 'I'm sorry' to me all the way out the door.

And I was left standing in the kitchen with Cameron's father.

My boss.

He knew damn well what we'd been doing. I had no work-related reason to be at his son's house for over twenty-four hours and yet, I still hadn't left. No point in denying it.

I looked at him and shrugged. He smiled.

I started to wash the dishes, and Mr. Fletcher, without a word, picked up a dishtowel and started to dry. I nodded to where Cameron and his mother were. "I take it Mrs. Fletcher took the news well."

He smiled. "She's known for years," he said, ever so casually. "Or so she said."

I thought she knew. The way she looked at me....

"She said a mother knows these things."

"Did you ever suspect anything?"

He shook his head. "I was... *we* were never sure," he answered honestly. "Truthfully, I considered he might be gay or at least bisexual."

"Why didn't you ever say something?"

"Because he wasn't ready," he answered. "And because it didn't matter."

"It *does* matter," I told him curtly. I looked at my boss and unclenched my jaw so I could speak. "Don't ever say it doesn't matter. It matters to him. He's been miserable for years."

He raised his hands defensively and grinned. "I meant it doesn't matter if he's gay or straight," he amended. "Lucas, if I'd have pushed him and he wasn't ready, he'd have denied it, and then he'd *never* come out. Sometimes, all a parent can do is support and love their kids. And wait."

I turned back to the sink and nodded. Then I sighed. Fuck. He was right. Cameron would have denied it. Vehemently.

Mr. Fletcher smiled at me. "Then you waltz into my office and tell me, in no uncertain terms, you're brilliant, successful and gay." He leaned against the kitchen counter and looked at me. "I'm not going to lie, Lucas, I'd hoped Cameron would see how it was possible... *if* he were gay."

I looked him straight in the eye. "Tell me honestly, did you hire me because I'm gay."

His eyes widened. "No! Absolutely not," he stated adamantly. "Lucas, I hired you because you're brilliant."

I believed him. I smiled. "It's true. I am."

He chuckled. "Although Cameron wasn't impressed.

We had many disagreements about your position at Fletcher Advertising."

"Is that so?" I said with a smile.

His father smirked, one corner of his lips lifting, just like Cameron. "I think he was threatened by you."

I smiled and shook my head. "I think it's because he likes me...."

Mr. Fletcher's eyes widened, and he stared out to where his son and wife were sitting. A slow smile spread across his face. "Oh."

I laughed. "So you thought pairing us up for the Lurex job would not only make him see how brilliant I am, but shake his closet until he fell out?"

He huffed out a laugh. "No, actually. We literally had sixty-five hours to put a campaign together, and I knew you two; how you work, how you think, would complement each other and get it done."

"Fair enough," I conceded with a smile. I let out the water and wiped down the sink.

Then Cameron's father said, "But you've been here longer than sixty-five hours..." he trailed off suggestively.

I looked him straight in the eye. "I have."

"You won't let this interfere with your job, will you," he made it a statement, rather than a question.

"No, Sir. I won't."

Then he asked me quietly. "You won't hurt him either, will you?"

I smiled, but then the thought occurred to me, maybe he wasn't the only one who'd get hurt. My smile died, I shook my head and my voice was quiet. "No, of course not."

Mr. Fletcher looked at me, and I avoided his eyes. "Lucas... I didn't mean to imply... oh God, I'm getting this all wrong."

"It's fine," I reassured him.

"No Lucas, please," he started again. "I just want him to be happy."

I looked at him, and I felt stripped bare. "So do I."

Just then, Cameron and his mom come back inside. He stopped and looked at me, then at his father, then back at me. "Everything okay?" he asked slowly.

His father smiled, but I answered. "Sure. I was just saying I have to get going."

"Oh," Cameron said, not convinced.

I told Mrs. Fletcher it was an absolute pleasure to see her again, and I told Mr. Fletcher I'd see him tomorrow at work. He smiled at me, with sorry in his eyes, and nodded. As I walked to the front door, I heard Cameron say, "I'll just walk Lucas out."

Then, from the hall, I heard Mrs. Fletcher hiss at her husband. "Tobias Fletcher, what did you say to him?"

I looked at Cameron, and he grimaced apologetically. As we walked to my car, he asked, "Did he say something to upset you?"

I smiled and shook my head, throwing my bag into the backseat. "Cameron, it's fine. He's concerned that's all, about his son, about his business."

Cameron looked kind of mortified. He looked back at his house then back to me, and his jaw clenched.

My voice was quiet. "He's worried I'm going to break your heart."

His eyes sparked and his mouth opened and closed two or three times. "I'm going to fucking kill him," he said. "I'm sorry. I'm sorry."

I grinned at him. "Don't worry, and don't apologize. Plus I think your mother's giving him what for right now." I opened my car door, and he started to walk back toward his house. "Cameron?" I called out to him. He turned to look at me, and I asked him, "Did you want to know what I told him?"

He looked at me questioningly.

"About me breaking your heart?" I clarified. He stared at me, waiting. I smiled at him. "I told him I wouldn't."

I got in my car and pulled out onto the street. When I looked in my rear vision mirror, he was still standing on the sidewalk.

He was still smiling.

18:00

I got home around 3 PM. I smiled when I could almost imagine that clock on Cameron's dresser would be on 18:00.

I unpacked my bags, including all the Lurex goodies I'd divvied up and claimed as mine. I opened my bedside drawer and threw everything in there, smiling when I saw the different types of condoms and flavored lubes. I laughed when I remembered Cameron channelling his inner Yoda with his glow-in-the-dark, green lightsabre.

And how he favored the strawberry scented lubricants, how he moaned when the prostate probe pressed deliciously against his gland, how his thighs would tremble, how his cock would twitch, what his come tasted like.

Mmm, God....

I quickly closed my bedside drawer and shook my head of all things Cameron. As many times as I'd had him, touched him, kissed him, sucked him, fucked him – had him inside me - it wasn't enough. I wanted more.

I knew. I *knew* I wanted more.

Not just sex, though. I wanted to hear him talk about global trends, financial reviews, cartoon socks, music, books and political hierarchies. I wanted to see him smile, hear him laugh.

And I knew, without a fucking doubt, I was in over my head.

Unable to stop thinking about him, I tried to busy myself with tidying up, and after I decided there was nothing in my kitchen to eat for dinner, I was bored and I felt as though my skin didn't fit right. I could smell him on me and I was restless because I wanted more of him, and I was getting agitated because I wasn't with him....

...then my doorbell buzzed.

Not expecting anyone, I pressed the intercom. "Who is it?"

"Cameron."

And I fucking grinned, so hard. I pressed the button. Hearing it click, I opened my front door and stood against it waiting for him. He stepped out of the lift and smiled when he saw me. He walked through my door, passed me without a word, and I kicked it closed behind me.

"Nice place," he said, looking around.

I was still smiling. "So what do I owe the pleasure?" He had a bag in his hand. I hadn't even noticed it. "Did I forget something?"

"A few things," he said. He reached into the bag, and then he held up a pair of socks. "They're plain black. They're *not* mine."

I chuckled, and we just stared at each other, both smiling like idiots. "So," I said, "your folks took the news okay? Your mom seemed happy, actually."

He nodded. "Yeah, they did. I even went and saw Ben."

I could feel my eyes widen. "How did that go?"

He smiled. "He stared and gaped for a while, but he's okay. I think I shocked him more than anything. He didn't say much," he said with a shrug. "I spoke with Ashley for a while, and before I left he asked me if all those times he'd taken me to the football, if I'd only gone to perv on men in tight pants... so I think he's okay."

"Did you?" I asked. "Only go to see all those sweaty men?"

"Oh absolutely," he said with a chuckle.

I smiled at him. "That's great, Cameron," he knew I was referring to his family accepting him. "That's really great."

"It is," he nodded.

"You weren't too hard on your dad, were you?"

He snorted. "I didn't say anything my mother already hadn't, apparently."

Laughing, I offered him a drink, and when I handed him a soda, he took a deep breath and said, "Um, about tomorrow...."

"What about it?"

"At work," he said, nervously. "What do we do... how do we... I don't know what...."

I put my can of soda on the kitchen counter and stepped in front of him. "I'm just going to be me, and you will be you. What we do at work won't change."

He exhaled, relieved.

"Cameron, I'm not going to kiss you in a staff meeting or anything," I teased him. "Unless you want me to."

He laughed, but I told him, "But I also don't want you to ignore me. I don't expect us to be anything less than professional, but I also don't want you to treat me like I mean nothing to you."

Fuck. Now I sounded like a girl.

His smile faded, and his eyebrows knitted together. "I won't. I don't think I *could* ignore you anymore." He looked at me, then to floor between us. "And outside of work...?"

"I told you I wanted to take you out," I reminded him. "And I meant it. I want to see you, Cam."

He bit his lip, to stop from smiling it would seem. "As in a date?"

"Yes, as in a date," I answered. Great. Now I was grinning *and* giddy like a girl. I cleared my throat and changed the subject. "So, you said I left a few things at your house?" He'd only showed me one.

He grinned, but a faint blush crept over his cheek. "Your tie," he said, reaching into the bag and throwing it onto the table. "I couldn't bring my countdown clock, but I did find this," he said, pulling out his phone. "I downloaded an app that might be useful." He held his phone up, showing me the screen. 14:29

A countdown clock on his phone. I laughed. "My dear man, you've thought of everything."

"I try." He grinned beautifully. Then he cleared his throat and reached back into the bag. "And there's this."

He pulled out the nude colored dildo. I barked out a laugh. "Um no," I corrected him. "That was yours. I called dibs on the black one, remember?"

He smiled, almost shyly. "Oh, no, it's mine," he said. "But you promised to do something with it, and you never did."

I smiled. Although I knew what he was referring to, I wanted to hear him say it. "What did I promise?"

"You um... you said you'd, um..." he stammered while his cheeks tinted pink.

So I stepped right up close and whispered in his ear. "Repeat after me..." I started. "I'm gonna fuck you with it."

His voice was coarse and barely a breath. "You're gonna fuck me with it."

"Then I'll lick you and suck you."

His chest heaved twice before he said it. "You'll lick me

and suck me."

"Then I'll rim you."

He swallowed. Twice. "You'll r-r-rim me."

I smiled against his ear. "Then I'll fuck you again."

He didn't finish, but he nodded against my neck. "Please."

14:03

There was no sight like it. Cameron was writhing and squirming, pushing his ass toward me. The dildo was embedded in his ass, I was between his legs, licking his cock, sucking on the head, and he was groaning beautifully.

His hands fisted the sheets at his side, his back arched, pushing himself onto the dildo, and he was begging for more. He was so beautiful. How he moved, how he moaned.

As fucking hot as it was to see him like this, I didn't want him to come until I was inside him. I slowly pulled the dildo out. He whined and looked at me like I'd lost my fucking mind.

I knelt up between his legs and, smoothing a condom down my aching length, I told him, "I want my cock to make you come."

His eyes rolled before they closed, and he whined and whimpered. I leaned down, licked his leaking slit and then swiped my tongue across his pink and open hole.

He almost screamed as he bucked into me, so I gripped his hips to hold him still. He opened his legs wider for me, and I flicked my tongue across his opening. The dildo had spread him well, my tongue slid in and out, and his thighs trembled. I knew he wouldn't last long.

So I grabbed the backs of his knees and leaned them forward, his ass was exposed and open.

I pressed my cock against his hole and slid inside him.

And he groaned. And moaned. And trembled. His head

pushed back into the pillows, and his chest pressed forward.

"Fuuuuuuuuuck," he groaned.

"Mmmmm," I agreed as I slid out and pushed back into him. He felt so fucking good. So hot, so deep and so fucking right. "I don't want the dildo to make you come," I panted to him. "Don't want anything else in your ass but me."

I thrust harder, and he moaned. "Yesssss."

"All of me," I told him as I pushed his legs higher, raising his ass for me. "Every inch," I moaned as I leaned over him, forcing every fucking inch of my cock inside him. He groaned, and I rocked us back and forth, my balls rubbing on his ass. "Every fucking inch," I grunted out. "My cock fucking you, making you come, nothing else... *nobody* else."

And his ass tightened around me. He trembled and bucked as he came, his cock emptying between us. He cried out and flexed against me, and my cock swelled and spilled. I bucked into him as I spurt hot and thick into the condom, lost in a show of fireworks behind my eyes.

We fell into a mass of sated, boneless bodies, wrapped around each other, and we slept.

3:16

I woke up to a scratchy feeling being rubbed across my lower back. It should have annoyed me.

But it didn't.

Because with the scratchy feeling was a soft, hot, wet feeling, that felt very fucking good.

I moaned, and heard a chuckle.

Then long, wide spread fingers were rubbing my back and the scratchy stubble and soft wet tongue were gliding from my spine to my ass crack.

Going lower.

And lower.

Oh, Jesus. Oh, fuck, he was about to....

Mmmm, he did it.

He fucking rimmed me. Long and hard.

Then he added his fingers. Not long after, the tip of the dildo was stretching me farther, and he fucked me.

Oh, God. How he fucked me.

I was lying face down, lifting my ass for him, and he buried the toy in me, sliding, twisting, pulling and pushing.

I slid my hand underneath me and grabbed my dick, pulling and twisting in time with his movements. And it was bliss, so fucking good. Then he did what I did to him.

He fucking took it out.

"Nooo," I shook my head, pleading with him. "Cameron, please..."

I could hear foil ripping, then a second's silence before he was inside me. Quick, hard and deep. "Is that what you want?" he whispered into the back of my neck.

All I could do was groan.

And nod.

And buck and spread my legs so he could fuck me harder.

And he did.

He pounded me into the mattress, fucking me for all he was worth.

It was glorious.

I lifted my hips and he gripped my shoulders, as his cock impaled me, over and over, relentlessly.

Perfectly.

His thrusts became irregular, and he rammed himself into me, roaring, spasming and erupting inside me.

I could feel his cock swell, I could feel every throb, it set fire to my cells, and my orgasm buckled me. I shuddered and writhed under him. My head fell back and snapped forward as my come smeared the sheets beneath me.

He collapsed on me, chuckling and gently rubbing his stubbled jaw across my skin.

All I could do was moan.

It wasn't even six thirty in the fucking morning.

"I have to go home," he said. "I need to get changed for work."

"Mm hmm," I moaned my no.

I could feel him smile against my shoulder. "Okay, shower first, *then* I have to go."

2:10

"The Road Runner?" I laughed.

He held up his other foot and grinned. "And Wiley E. Coyote."

I shook my head at him and laughed as he slipped his shoes on. "I have to go," he said again. He looked at his watch. "I'll see you in two hours."

"Yeah, yeah, fuck me and leave," I said sarcastically, rolling my eyes at him.

He barked out a laugh. "You can return the favor any time."

I grinned. "I think I will."

"Good," he said, with a quick peck to my lips. He walked to the door, turned and said, "This weekend, you can fuck me and leave several times over."

I laughed. "Starting?"

"Friday night," he said, and the door closed behind him.

I'd never been so happy to go to work.

00:10

I couldn't have timed it better, because when I stepped into the elevator, among other people, was Cameron. He smiled smugly when he saw me. I looked at him, wondering how this would work between us when his lips twitched. He said, "And how are you this morning?"

I smiled. "Oh, I was excellent this morning. Or so I was told."

He pouted, to stop from smiling, but his eyes shone.

The elevator stopped, and our fellow passengers got out leaving Cameron and I to travel the final few floors alone. He looked at me. "Do you feel okay? You're not too sore?"

I smiled at his concern. "I am a little," I told him honestly. "And I *really* want you to do it again."

He smiled. "Good."

"Cameron, can I ask you something?"

He looked taken aback by my question.

Just as the elevator stopped and the doors open at our floor, I asked him, "Who's on your socks?"

He grinned and we stepped out into the hall, walking toward our offices. "Superman."

I smiled. "With Clark Kent?"

He got to his door. "No. Just Superman," he said with a grin. "No need for Clark anymore."

We walked into our respective offices, and when I sat at my desk, I looked through the glass wall. He spun his chair around, looked at me through the glass wall and grinned.

Rachel's voice scared the shit out of me. "Well, you look rather pleased with yourself."

I clutched at my heart. "Jeez, Rach. You gave me a heart attack."

She smiled and handed me a coffee. "And someone else," she gave a pointed glance to the room across the hall, "seems to have found himself some swagger."

I looked at her and laughed. "That's me," I said, taking a sip of my coffee. "The giver of swagger."

Four Weeks Later

My desk phone buzzed, it was Mr. Fletcher's office. I pressed the flashing button. "Lucas, my office in five, please."

I looked at my watch. It was 3:45 PM on Wednesday. A little odd for an unscheduled meeting. I tidied up my desk, putting files to one side and closed down my laptop.

I opened my office door at the same time Cameron opened his. He pointed toward his father's office, and I nodded.

"Do you know what it's about?" I asked.

He smiled. "Yeah, maybe he's still upset about you eating the leftover pie on Sunday."

I snorted. "Your mom makes good pie."

He chuckled, and we walk into his father's office. Mr Fletcher looked at us both and smiled. "Take a seat, boys."

We did as he asked, he leaned back in his chair and put his pen down. "Fletcher Advertising has a meeting with Caiusaro on Tuesday at 10 AM. They're an Italian company looking to break into the American market."

"What's the product?" I asked.

But it was Cameron who answers. "Socks."

I almost fucking laughed. I had to bite the inside of my lip so I didn't.

"It's a lucrative deal," Mr. Fletcher went on to say. "I want you both to work on it. You have more time. Six days to be exact, so after Lurex, I don't think that'll be a problem."

I quickly did the math in my head.

One hundred and sixty two hours.

"No problem at all," I said. I looked at Cameron and grinned. "My place. I'll bring the whiteboard, you bring the clock."

EPILOGUE

"I don't want to go," I mumbled into the back of his neck. "I want to stay here." I kissed and nipped at the skin behind his ear, hoping my powers of persuasion could convince him.

"Just like this," I said, sucking his delectable skin between my lips. "All day, all night."

He moaned and chuckled, and I could feel his chest vibrate underneath me. He might just be lying face down, and I might just be lying on top of him. We may be lying naked in bed. We may have just finished making love.

And I still wanted more of him.

I would always want more of him.

"We have to go," he murmured. "It's a special thing. Dad even invited other people from work."

"But it's Saturday..." I whined.

I may have been sulking, quite possibly even pouting.

"Mom made pie," he said with a smile in his voice.

I fell against him heavily and sighed. "You don't play fair."

He laughed again and tried to turn over so he could face

me. I pushed up, giving him room to move, but quickly settled myself back on top of him, between his legs.

With my elbow beside his chest, I propped my head on my hand and looked at him. He had bed hair, a sated gaze and a blissful smirk; his post coital glow. He was fucking beautiful.

He reached up and pushed the hair off my face. "How did I ever get so lucky?" he wondered out loud.

"Don't you remember?" I teased him. "Six months ago you made me spend the weekend – and you showed me your feet." I rolled my eyes and sighed dramatically. "I was done for."

He chuckled. "Oh, that's right," he said, rolling his eyes back at me.

"Anyway," I said, trailing my fingertips along his eyebrow, around the corner of his eye, across his cheekbone. "I'm not exactly too unlucky either."

He smiled, and there was love in his eyes. Then he rolled us over so he was on top of me.

"Flattery will get you laid, but it won't get you out of lunch at Mom and Dad's."

I went back to pouting. "I'd still rather stay here."

He grinned. "Me too, baby," he said, sliding off me. He walked to his bedroom door and said, "But we can't. We have to go. I'm showering first, and I'm locking the door. If you join me, we'll never leave."

I snorted, and he grinned.

He knew all my tricks.

I heard the shower start, and I didn't doubt he'd locked the bathroom door. He knew me well. The thought made me smile.

Every single thought I had of him made me smile. Even when we fought or disagreed--he was particularly fiery and sexy when he was pissed off, and the make-up sex was particularly delicious.

I even smiled as I remembered our first fight. We'd been 'together' non-stop for about four weeks. We'd done the Lurex deal, we'd spent nearly every day together at work, every night together as well. Then we'd had the Caiusaro campaign, where we'd spent another six full days and nights together. We had two days off after we secured the Caiusaro campaign, which we spent together. By the second day, we needed a break.

We'd argued over peanut butter fucking ice cream.

Of all the things.

It was trivial and stupid. I'd yelled, and then he'd yelled. I said some things I shouldn't have, and he returned the favor. He slammed a door, so I stormed out. I got home and spent the entire night tossing and turning, apparently unable to sleep a wink without him. The door buzzer woke me around eight the next morning; with a groan and a hollow, heavy lump in my chest, I pressed the intercom. "Who is it?"

"It's me," was all he said.

I pressed the button to let him in. When he got to my door, I could see he'd spent a night similar to mine. "I'm sorry," he said. "I don't want to fight."

"Me either," I answered. "I'm sorry, too. I'm sorry I said those things. I mean really, I don't give a fuck about ice cream."

He chuckled and pulled me against his chest, where I fit just right. It made me sigh.

He pulled away from me, kissed me lightly and said he was going home, he just wanted to apologize. He thought after spending so much time together, it was best if we spent the last day of our weekend by ourselves doing whatever.

As much as I didn't want to, I knew he was right.

And so I spent the rest of the day wondering what the fuck I did with my life before Cameron Fletcher.

I cleaned and did some laundry, then went for a walk - for coffee, for something to do. The barista tried to make small talk, asking me a slew of questions and smiling.

It wasn't until I'd walked two blocks with my coffee in hand I realized he'd hit on me. Now Lucas Hensley, pre-Cameron, would have been onto that. He'd have smiled, flirted and secured a possible regular fuck. But now Lucas Hensley, post-Cameron, didn't even realize.

And it occurred to me as I got to my building, I haven't even looked at another guy.

Not one. Not once. Not ever.

Not since Cameron.

I should have known then the 'L word' wasn't far away. In hindsight, I should have fucking seen it coming.

I just didn't expect it to come from my mother.

I'd organized a four day weekend to go back home to visit my mom. I was arranging dates with her over the phone when she'd demanded to speak to Cameron.

Then she'd demanded he come with me to see her.

Cameron had mumbled, "I um... I um...."

And my Momma had declared it was settled. She'd see us both at the airport, and Cameron handed me back my phone. The poor guy didn't know what to say. I think he was too scared to say no. After I'd got off the phone to Momma, I'd told him he was under no obligation to go. His only response was, "So your inability to take no for an answer is hereditary, right?"

But then he'd said he'd never been to Texas, and so a month later we both boarded a plane for Dallas. We'd enjoyed a late lunch on Momma's back porch as she asked

Cameron a hundred-and-one questions. I stood up to clear away the table, and she looked up at me and smiled. "I can see why you love him," she said.

I blinked and my mouth opened, and then it closed. I repeated this action a couple of times I think, trying to say something, but I couldn't make a sound. I looked at Cameron's wide eyes, then to my mother's fading smile.

Momma stood up. "Lucas Hensley! You've never told him?"

"Momma..." I whispered.

"I know you, Son. I can see how you look at him." She put her hand on her hip. "Do you deny it?" she asked me outright, right in front of him.

I looked at Cameron, still sitting there, wide eyed, a little pale and whole lot of hopeful.

I couldn't deny it. I shook my head no.

"You *do* love him," Momma announced, and all I could do was look at Cameron. And nod.

Because I did.

I loved him.

Momma beamed, and walked inside mumbling something about silly boys, silly boys. And then Cameron was standing in front of me, and his hand was touching my cheek. "Luc," he whispered.

I looked at him then, knowing he'd see nothing but honesty in my eyes. I nodded, because it was all I could do. He grinned a heart stopping grin, pulled me into his arms and whispered into my ear that he'd waited so God damn long to hear that. He said he knew I did love him.

He could see it, he wasn't blind. He told me he'd been in love with me since forever and was just waiting until I was ready.

He said he knew it was new to me, and he could wait,

he didn't mind. He'd wait forever if he had to. When I found my voice, I told him, whispered soft in his ear, that I think I fell for him that very first weekend.

When my Momma walked back outside to where we were, we were both grinning and giggling, and somewhat handsy. If I wasn't at my Momma's, or if she wasn't home, I'd have had him on the back porch table.

Or begged him to have me.

That entire weekend we couldn't get enough of each other. I had to be touching him at all times, just touching or near him at least. And at night, we made love for hours, we barely slept a wink. He'd whisper his love for me, moaning into my neck as he pushed himself into me. And I'd whisper the words out loud, just for him, as I slid inside him, and again as we'd wrap ourselves around the other falling into sleep.

Texas was two months ago, and we'd been like that ever since. Not at work, of course. But when it was just us, it was really *just us*.

"What are you smiling about?" Cameron's voice startled me back to the present.

"Texas." That's all I had to say. He grinned beautifully in understanding.

"Now go get showered," he ordered, still smiling. "Or we'll be late."

I rolled off the bed and stood in front of him, stark naked, my cock heavy and limp – and waiting. I was pretending to yawn and stretch and scratch my head, but really I was just giving him ample time to check me out and hopefully change his mind.

"Luc," he threatened. "I know what you're doing. It's not going to work."

I pouted and sulked all the way to the shower. He really did know all my tricks.

———

"Is it really just smart casual?" I asked, unsure if I'll be underdressed.

"Yes, Luc," Cameron answers, again. "It's just lunch."

I sat on his sofa. "I hope you don't mind, I had to borrow some socks," I told him. "I left mine at my place."

We still had our own places. We agreed working and living together might be a little too much too soon. Not that I saw much of my place....

"Who did you get?" he asked, looking at the socks.

"Pooh and Tigger," I told him. "I couldn't find the striped ones from Aunt Nae."

He grinned and pulled his jean leg up so I could see different stripes of green on the socks I had been looking for. I hadn't particularly wanted to wear cartoon socks.

"They're my new favorite," he said without shame.

When we'd visited Momma, her good friend, who I'd always addressed as my Aunt, was knitting socks. Fine, silk-like cotton socks. Cameron was in his weird-sock-fettish-heaven, except he didn't want plain black ones.

No, of course not.

He'd put in an order for funny colored, stripey ones. Two socks of every kind of green imaginable arrived in the mail two weeks later. He had since sent her money to make him some more.

Of all the colors he could think of, apparently.

I put on Pooh and Tigger and said a silent prayer I didn't have to take off my boots.

As we pulled up at the front of Cameron's parents' house, I asked him, "Any idea what this lunch is for?"

Cameron shook his head. "No, all I know is Dad got into his office yesterday, checked his mail, made some phone calls and ten minutes later he told me we had to be here at twelve sharp."

As we walked to the front door, I pointed to a familiar Mercedes. "Hey, isn't that Webber's car?"

Cameron nodded and frowned, looking at other cars parked nearby. "Bromley and Otterski are here too," he said.

All the executives.

Fuck.

"Something big must have happened," Cameron said quietly.

"Hey," I said softly. "Are you okay?"

"Sure," he answered. "Why wouldn't I be?"

"Just with us, walking in here together, that's all."

He smiled. "Luc, at work they don't need to know about us, because we don't flaunt our relationship, and because it's none of their business." Then he said, "But we're *not* at work, this is my parents' house. If they don't like it, they can go to fucking hell."

I laughed and smiled proudly.

He opened the front door and held it open for me. "I learned from the best," he said with a smirk.

"That you did, baby."

We walked into the open lounge area that joins the kitchen. "Oh, hi boys," Mrs. Fletcher greeted us from across the room.

I noticed Paul Bromley and Eric Newton eyeing us, smiling falsely, wondering why the hell we'd just arrived together. I gave them a small nod on my way to Cameron's mother, and their eyes widened when I kissed her cheek.

I asked her if there was anything I could do to help, but she smiled beautifully and told me no, don't be silly dear. There were a few other people from work, Rachel and Simona included. There were some hired wait staff offering hors d'oeuvres and drinks, so I grabbed two beers off a tray and walked over to where Cameron was talking with the two girls and handed him one.

Simona and Rachel had no idea as to the purpose of this meeting either, and they were surprised we didn't know. "We were going to ask you!" Rachel said. "But it has to be something important because Tweedle Dumb and Tweedle Even Dumber are here," she said, nodding pointedly at Paul and Eric.

"They do look a little pleased with themselves," Cameron conceded, taking a drink of his beer.

"Maybe they think they have a chance with two pretty, single ladies...." I looked at them suggestively.

"Bromley's a sleaze," Simona said with a shudder.

Rachel nodded vehemently. "And Newton would prefer either of you two rather than Simona or I."

What?

I looked at Eric. *He was gay?* How could I have missed *that?*

"He's *gay?*" I asked quietly.

Both girls *and* Cameron nodded.

Right. That's it. I've lost my touch. More than slightly peeved, I looked at Cameron. "You broke my gay-dar."

"I *what?*" he scoffed, while Simona snorted back her drink and proceeded to choke. I went to grab her a napkin, or something, off the servery just as Mr. Fletcher called for everyone's attention. I was standing across the room from Cameron, next to Bromley and Newton of all people, and we all turned to face our boss.

Standing next to the baby grand piano, Mr. Fletcher thanked us all for giving up our Saturday, but this news, in his very humble opinion couldn't wait.

"I received a confirmation telephone call yesterday from an old friend of mine in France," he said.

Okaaaay. A little odd for sharing that tidbit of news with all of us, but thanks.

"...in Cannes, actually."

Cannes.

Why should that ring a bell?

I looked at Cameron. His eyes were wide, but he was starting to smile. He got the significance.

What was I missing?

Mr. Fletcher picked up a remote control, and pointing it at the large flat screen, he turned it on. He looked at his watch and announced, "It's almost time."

And then, right on cue, on screen, a well-dressed man announced with a thick European accent, "We present to you, this year's winner of the Cannes Lion!"

It was funny how the monumental shit in your life tends to happen in slow-motion and at warp speed at the same time. Because on the screen appeared a lonely little sock puppet; a real sock on an animated background.

And my mind seemed to fracture. I could recall the hours upon fucking hours it took with animators, our CGI team, even puppeteers. I could recall the hours upon fucking hours it took with Cameron to get it absolutely perfect. I could see, all around me, as people were grinning and clapping, offering congratulations, and I could see Cameron across the room.

He was looking at the screen, and then at me, then back to the screen.

I could see all this. A blur of soundless commotion,

moving in slow-motion, while my mind recalled specific split-second details of the advertisement we were watching.

But my mind couldn't seem to make the leap that the man said "winner of the Cannes Lion" and then showed our Caiusaro sock ad.

I couldn't seem to join the dots.

Winner.

Cannes Lion.

The annual award for the best ad in the world.

Fletcher Advertising.

Our ad.

Mine and Cameron's ad.

The ad features a sad and lonely little puppet sock, in a drab, colorless world, who appears to be looking for something he's lost. He passes pretty socks, even handsome socks, but shakes his head and keeps walking. He does look twice at one particular colorful, striped sock – which Cameron insisted on and still found hilarious - but this poor little sock just can't find what he is looking for.

Unable to go on, he is just about to pull a thread to unravel himself, when a cartoon ambulance pulls up, the doctor-socks grabs him, lays him on a gurney and rushes him away. The doctors perform CPR, and when they hit him with paddles, his little sock back arches off the bed. Finally the ambulance doors open, and the animated world is bright and colourful, Wizard of Oz style.

"Where am I?" the sock asks.

"Caiusaro," a soft voice answers. "It's Heaven for socks. Heaven for feet."

We had three other sock ads to follow, showing a different sock each time on their adventure to get to Caiusaro. We had over seven million hits on Youtube, our twitter feed of Where Is Cauisaro? even trended worldwide.

The ad finished on screen – it had only been thirty seconds – and then Cameron was grinning and walking toward me. Then he was laughing and holding my face and planted one on me, right there, in front of everyone.

"Cannes?" I said, though it was more of a squeak.

He laughed and nodded, wrapping his hand around the back of my neck and pulling me against him. We were then joined by Rachel and Simona who were jumping and hugging us.

Then we were somehow apart, and other people were congratulating us.

I was in a fucking daze, vaguely aware of Cameron's father talking. "We knew Cameron and Lucas's Caiusaro ad had been nominated, along with twenty-eight thousand of the world's best advertisements," he said. Then Mr. Fletcher looked between his son and me and announced proudly, "There will be an official award ceremony, but the phone call I took was from the Managing Director to tell me you'd won."

Oh.

My.

Fucking.

God.

Cameron looked at me, still smiling. "You okay?" he asked.

I nodded, I think. I wasn't completely sure, to be honest.

I looked around then and saw some people were smiling, and some couldn't hide their surprise at Cameron kissing me. Like Eric and Paul. I wasn't sure what was wider – their mouths or their eyes.

But Cameron just grabbed my hand and led me toward

where was father was standing, and I realized people were chanting, "speech, speech."

Well, Simona and Rachel were chanting, "speech, speech."

Cameron was beaming, and he thanked the teams which worked with us and he thanked Simona and Rachel, who were worth their weight in gold. He talked of his dreams when he was a boy to have a Cannes Lion, just like his dad. And now he'd done it. He said it should be the pinnacle of a career, an award like this, but he thought it was just the beginning.

He looked at me when he said he was certain they hadn't seen the best of what we could do.

Then it was my turn to talk, but I didn't know what to say. These people were used to seeing the business side of me, the arrogant side of me.

Not many people had ever seen the humbled side of me.

I was a little lost for words, they seemed to be stuck in my throat. "I um," I started poorly. I exhaled through puffed cheeks. "I can't really explain..." I told them. "I had no idea..." I was stammering like a fool, so I took a deep breath and started again. "When I started with Fletcher Advertising twelve months ago, I knew what I could give. I knew what Fletcher Advertising would get from me."

Mr. Fletcher laughed. "Yes," he told the small audience. "He told me in his interview if in twelve months he'd not increased our portfolio by twenty-five percent, I could kick his ass or fire it."

"It's true, I did say that." I grinned and nodded. "But for all the things I knew I could give, I never dreamed of what I'd be getting in return." I looked at Cameron, and he knew I wasn't just talking about work. He smiled.

"But Cameron's right," I admitted. "I really think it's just the beginning of what we're capable of."

Cameron grinned and again, in front everyone, we had one of those just-us moments.

Mr. Fletcher then talked to the small audience in front of us, though I wasn't really listening. I was still trying to get my head around winning the fucking Cannes Lion, and Cameron kissing me in front of co-workers.

Then Mr. Fletcher said, "Originally, I was going to have today's lunch at some fancy restaurant, but it just didn't seem right. It needed to be personal, because that's what this is. To me," Cameron's father said looking at Cameron first, then at me, with shining eyes, "it's very personal."

We were each handed a glass of champagne, and Mr. Fletcher asked us to raise our glasses.

He lifted his glass in a toast. "To two of the best minds in the business, and to two of the best men I know."

I looked at Cameron, and he was already looking at me. His voice was quiet, but I heard him just fine. "To us."

I nodded and whispered, just for him. "To us."

The crowd drank and conversations started to buzz between the small groups. Mr Fletcher embraced Cameron, and then to my utter surprise, he did the same to me.

"I'm so proud of both of you," he told us. Mrs. Fletcher was there hugging us both, telling us how very proud and happy she was.

Then a grinning Ben clapped us both on the back and hugged us both at the same time so damn tight my spine cracked.

"Jeez, Ben," I complained. "Thanks for the spinal alignment."

He grinned. "Just helping. You know, so you're both all limber for later on."

Cameron rolled his eyes, Cynthia scowled at her eldest son, and I laughed. Ben just shrugged and grinned. Then he looked at me, and said, rather loudly, "Got a little choked up before, Lucas?"

I smiled, a little embarrassed, and nodded. "Um yeah, Cameron had just told me how your mom had made a pecan pie just for me and how no one else was to have any." I put my hand to my heart, "I was touched."

Ben gasped and glared at his mother, while Cameron slid his arm around my waist, and chuckling, pressed his lips to my temple. But then Mr. Fletcher looked at his wife. "You told me I could have some! After lunch, you said 'the pie's for after lunch'."

Mrs. Fletcher pursed her smiling lips at me, and Cameron laughed. He led me away from his still-bickering-about-pie family. "Come on, we better mingle."

So we did. We chatted with everyone; Paul and Eric included. They were a little surprised, to say the least. But they both wished us well and warm congratulations on the Lion win.

Soon it was mid-afternoon, the crowd had dissipated and there was just family left.

We were sitting at the outdoor table and Cameron's hand was on my thigh. We were enjoying the afternoon sun and pecan pie when Ashley asked how it felt to have won such a prestigious award.

"To be honest, I still don't think it's sunk in," I told her. "It was like it hasn't really happened."

Mr. Fletcher stood up and grinned. "Maybe this will help?" And he threw a dark blue, rectangular envelope onto the table in front of us.

Cameron picked it up and opened it. It was two airline tickets. To France.

I looked at Mr. Fletcher. And grinning, he explained, "Two tickets. You have two nights in Cannes, where you'll attend a ceremony to receive the award, and then you have four nights in Paris."

Oh.

I looked at Cameron, and he was grinning, so excited. "Paris?"

Paris.

I was going to Paris. With Cameron.

He leaned over and kissed me. His eyes were bright, and he was so fucking beautiful when he was happy.

And that choked-up, emotional lump appeared in my throat again. Fuck. I was turning into a girl.

I was all love hearts and flowers, and 'I love you's' and cuddling. First, Cameron broke my gay-dar, then he turned me into an emotional sap.

Maybe I should take Cameron home and fuck him. Fuck him until he was a writhing, moaning, begging, screaming mess. Then I wouldn't feel like such a fucking girl.

Or, maybe he could make love to me, hold me and kiss me, surging inside me as his eyes and his body told me without words just how much he loved me.

"Luc?"

"Oh, sorry," I apologized, taking a deep breath, shaking my head. "I zoned out there."

"Have you ever been to France?" Mr. Fletcher asked.

I shook my head and looked at Cameron. "I've always wanted to go."

He grinned and squeezed my thigh. "Me too."

Then Mrs. Fletcher asked, "I've always been meaning to ask, what was the inspiration for the Caisuaro ad? That little sock was so cute."

I grinned. "Well, crazy socks and foot fetishes... There was never a doubt. It was always going to be a perfect match."

I looked at Cameron, he smiled and said, "Never a doubt."

The End

OUTTAKE

TOBIAS'S POV OF THE MEETING WITH LUREX AND
WHAT HAPPENS AFTER.

"Watching them is like watching water and oil do the impossible."

As the three Lurex associates were being led in, I grabbed Rachel and Simona. "Girls, come on," I said, unable to hide my excitement. I led them into my office and opened the cabinet housing the monitors that feed the CCTV.

I switched all four screens to the conference room, and we stood and watched as Cameron and Lucas shook hands and made introductions to the team of three.

My adrenaline was pumping. This was what it was about. This was what I missed.

These days my time was spent in board meetings, press conferences, finance meetings. But my heart was in advertising. It was what I loved.

It was what I was good at.

It was why Fletcher Advertising was what it was.

The girls beside me buzzed excitedly. They didn't get to see their bosses do this. Most pitches were sold at the recipient's offices, behind closed doors. They put in the ground work and research but never got to see the boys do their thing.

The two girls were transfixed by the screens, watching, listening.

Cameron started. I watched him. He had an air of self-assuredness, a quiet confidence in the way he talked, the way he moved. He had *poise*. Like he could take on the world.

He reminded me of me.

A twenty-five years younger version of me.

Simona's voice beside me echoed my thoughts. "God, he's good."

I couldn't help but smile.

And then Lucas talked. He was so different from Cameron. Their methods, their approach, their expertise were so different. I knew pairing them together would be risky, but if they could see past their differences they'd make a damn good team.

Each man, by their own rights, was talented. Of that there was no doubt. But together... well, together they'd be unstoppable. Where Cameron's confidence was reserved, Lucas's confidence was out there for the world to see.

He had a cockiness, a smug certainty in everything he did, but it was his charm. It was difficult not to like him. Though Cameron seemed not to like him when Lucas had first started at Fletcher Advertising, he chose to ignore him rather than see him as an asset to the team.

I remember once, I'd confronted Cameron not long after Lucas had started. I'd asked him to put his differences aside.

Cameron had scoffed. "Differences?"

His reaction had baffled me at the time. Of course they had differences. "Look Cameron," I'd said. "You're both talented-"

"It's not that, Dad," he'd said quietly, then his cell phone rang, he took the call, and we never got back to the conversation. Cameron had always been quiet. Not un-happy, but never... I don't know... never at peace with himself.

Cameron's an intelligent, well-adjusted man. He has friends, both male and female, but we'd never seen him *with* someone. I knew he worked hard, I was the first to know what that was like. He put enough pressure on himself to succeed, so Cynthia and I had never really pushed him on his personal life.

He worked for the family business. He didn't need me adding pressure to his life outside of work as well. Whatever his options were, whatever his inclinations were, he'd tell us when he was ready.

Then I made him and Lucas spend the weekend together. When we'd called in to Cameron's yesterday morning to see them, things between them still seemed tense. I thought I'd made a mistake in pairing them together, though when we left, Cynthia had assured me they'd be just fine. She didn't seem concerned, in fact, she seemed rather pleased. So I let it go.

But something between these two men had changed.

Because just this morning, right before the meeting, I'd walked into Cameron's office to find them laughing. To find Cameron laughing. He looked so happy I'd almost forgotten what I went in to his office to tell them.

That the Lurex team had arrived. It was time to put sixty-five hours of hard work on the table.

And that was exactly what they did. And it was incredible. Watching them was like watching water and oil do the impossible.

They mixed.

They worked off each other, reading body language, invisible cues, as though they'd practiced a script. The pitch rolled seamlessly, like they'd done this together a thousand times.

They revealed their concept boards. We could see them clearly enough from the monitor, clear enough to see what they were.

Six boards; three pairs, two couples, one message.

On one hand, I was surprised they'd chosen to push the gay market, and on the other hand, I wasn't surprised at all. It was risky; it was a hard sell.

It was damn good.

Cameron was quick to point out percentages and figures, but it wasn't what he was saying that has me intrigued. It was how he was saying it. He had his back to them, looking out the window as he spoke.

"Cameron, what are you doing?" Simona whispered beside me. "Turn around."

I grinned. "He doesn't need to look at them. He's not selling them anything," I explained. "He's teaching them. He's showing them he has absolute faith in what he's saying."

Both girls looked at me, then back to the screen. "Oh, my God," Rachel said quietly.

Simona added, "That's brilliant."

"Yes, it is," I agreed. Then I amended, "*He* is."

And he was. He was brilliant. Pride warmed me through. I wished Cynthia was here. I wished his mom could see him like this.

Then Lucas asked if he could show them some footage, explaining it wasn't exactly suitable for "delicate ears." The well-dressed woman smiled and told him it was fine.

Rachel folded her arms. "He's such a charmer."

Simona giggled. "He doesn't even know he does it."

Rachel huffed and smiled. "Oh, he knows he does it, alright," she said. Then she stared closer at the screen. "Is that *Lucas* in that video? In that nightclub, with*out* a shirt?"

The three of us all leaned in. Yep. That was Lucas. Shirtless. Handing out condoms to a crowd of half-dressed men by the looks of it. I nodded. "Yep," I said with a grin. "It sure is."

We watched as the footage rolled, Lucas asking direct marketing questions. He was brilliant. The concept was in-your-face and real, and his audience, both on screen and sitting in front of him right now, were captivated. How very Lucas.

Then Cameron started. He turned around the two remaining concept boards showing two gaunt and sickly people. The change between this approach and the previous concept boards was vast.

Cameron ran more footage of the same two people, telling us how as little as one dollar cost them more than their health.

The audience of three on the monitor, and the two girls beside, me were quiet. Proof right there, the approach would work.

It was a shock concept. It was quiet, restrained, yet at the same time, it was high impact.

How very Cameron.

Then the boys closed ranks and discussed on-line options, tools and possibilities. They told them what they were doing now wasn't good enough and their competition was catching them. They told them in no uncertain terms a company in the 21st century couldn't afford *not* to move, change, evolve.

Not a second wasted, not a moment lost.

It was beautiful to watch.

And then the shorter of the two Lurex men, Mr. Vladimir, ignorantly questioned why Lurex should use Fletcher Advertising.

"What a dick," Simona mumbled. Then she looked at me. "Sorry."

I smiled. The little, funny looking man was a dick. "It's okay. He is a... one of those."

Both girls giggled. We watched Cameron tell Mr. Vladimir he should use Fletcher advertising so he didn't have to go back to his shareholders and tell them he was the reason they lost money.

God damn. I laughed, because it was something I'd say. Hell, it was something I've even said.

But then the boss, Mr. Makenna asked his colleagues to leave.

"What's he doing?" Rachel looked at me.

I answered quietly, honestly. "I don't know."

When the other two had left the room, the older man asked, "Are you always so confident?"

Both Cameron and Lucas answered in unison. "Yes."

I smiled, Simona and Rachel both snorted.

Then Makenna told them he was impressed, but he had doubts. He liked the idea, he liked the direction, but he was just not convinced. "...just *how* sure are you this gay aspect will work?"

Lucas started to speak, but Cameron cut him off. "I know this will work, Mr. Makenna," he said as his eyes dart to the CCTV camera, like he was checking to see if we were watching. He turned back to the man in front of him and said, "I know this will work, because I'm gay."

I heard one of the girls gasp... Simona, I think. Her hand grabbed Rachel's arm on reflex. But I couldn't take my eyes off the screen. I stepped closer to it. Cameron was staring straight at the camera.

He was looking straight at me.

I'm gay, he said.

Just like that.

For one long second, he stared at me.

This wasn't part of the campaign. This wasn't some ploy to sell a pitch. This was real.

I'd seen that look on his face before. I just couldn't place it. That haunted, vulnerable, please-forgive-me look.... he was little when I last saw that look on his face.

On screen, he turned back to Makenna and wrapped up the meeting. But I couldn't pay attention. Makenna was smiling and shaking their hands, and I think it was a done deal. I think they'd scored the Lurex contract.

But it wasn't important.

Cameron's face. *Please-forgive-me....*

He was just a kid. I remember... he was playing in my study, he was pretending to be me at my desk. He swung around on the swivel chair and knocked the crystal inkwell to the ground, breaking it. It was my father's.

When I came home, he confronted me, all on his own, claiming responsibility.

I'm so sorry, Daddy. Please forgive me.

The look on his face.

I'm so sorry, Daddy. Please forgive me.

I made my feet work and walked to the double doors. I wasn't even sure if Makenna was still in there. I didn't care if he was.

Because suddenly a twenty million dollar contract didn't mean a thing.

Cameron and Lucas were alone, and they turned to look at me. Cameron looked at me. He looked so scared. No, no, no, no, no....

Lucas's asked him something. Did he want him to stay? And the look on Cameron's face broke my heart. He was scared.

He was scared of me.

But again like he was eight years old, he told Lucas no. He'd do this on his own.

And he wasn't a grown man. He was my son. He was my little boy all over again. And I made my feet work again and rushed over to him - this scared little boy - and hugged him.

He froze for a moment before he hugged me back. I threaded my fingers through the hair at his collar and held him, and his arms squeezed me in return.

"Oh, Cameron," I said. "Please don't be scared," I whispered to him as I hugged him. He didn't answer, so I asked him, "Are you okay?"

He nodded, and I pulled back and looked at him, expecting to find tears. But the only tears were mine.

"Are you?" he asked quietly.

"Better than okay," I told him, wiping my cheeks. "Cameron, I'm so proud of you. What you did just now, what you told him..."

"Was reckless," he offered softly.

"What?" I asked. "Cameron, it was the bravest thing I've ever seen. It took guts."

He looked down at the floor, and I stopped him. "I'll have none of that," I told him, lifting his face up with both of my hands. "Keep your chin up, Son. Don't apologize. Don't look down for anyone."

His eyes. God, his eyes. He was still so unsure. "Dad... is it really okay? You don't mind... that... that I'm gay?"

"Of course it's okay," I told him. "I just want you to be happy, Cameron. Your mother and I, we just want you to be happy."

He rubbed his temples. "Oh, God. Mom..."

"I can tell her," I offered.

He nodded. "I will call her," he said. He said he needed some time, needed some sleep. He knew his mom would have questions, hundreds of them, and he just wanted some time to adjust, to get his head around it. "I'm tired, Dad," he said. And he looked it. "You can tell her; I don't expect you to lie to her. Just tell her I'll call her after I've slept more than eight hours in three days."

"Of course," I reassured him.

"Do you think she'll be okay with it, Dad?" He looked out the window, and his voice was so quiet. "I don't want to disappoint her."

"Cameron, look at me." My voice was soft but serious. I waited until his eyes meet mine before I told him, "Your mother just wants you to be happy. You watch," I said with a smile. "She'll be President of PFLAG before Christmas."

I couldn't help but laugh, and it made him smile. He was quiet, not withdrawn, but more reflective I think. "You look exhausted, Son. You should go home."

He exhaled through puffed out cheeks, and then he

nodded. "Yeah. I'm tired." He stood up straight from leaning against the table.

"Cameron," I told him. "Before we leave this room, you need to know, what happens out there," I motioned to the world on the other side of the door. "I'll support you. If you want to tell the whole wide world, I'll be behind you. Whatever you decide."

He ran his hand through his hair. "Thanks, Dad. But can we just take it one day at a time?"

"Sure," I told him. "Of course we can." I walked to the door.

"Dad?" He called out to stop me. I turned, and he looked me straight in the eye. "Can I ask you something?"

My hand fell from the door handle, and I gave him my full attention. "Of course."

"You watched the whole Lurex pitch, didn't you?"

I nodded.

"Lucas's um..." he started quietly. "He's um...he's..." His words trailed away, unfinished.

"He's what, Cameron?"

"Just promise me, no matter what happens... after today... you won't send him back to Texas."

Texas? "Why on *Earth* would I do that?"

"No reason," he smiled. "I know I've given you a hard time about him working here. But," he took a deep breath and exhaled loudly. "But he's brilliant, Dad. There's no way I could have gotten the Lurex contract on my own."

"I doubt either of you could have done it on your own, Cameron." I couldn't help but chuckle. "Unless you're Superman underneath that Armani suit."

Cameron smiled, a genuine, tired smile. Then he laughed and shook his head. "More than you know, Dad."

"Come on," I told him with a smile and opened the door.

"Let's go find the other half of your dynamic duo. Even superheroes need to sleep, Cameron."

I walked out the door, heading for Lucas's office, and I heard Cameron's quiet voice behind me. "They sure do, Dad."

The Very End

ABOUT THE AUTHOR

N.R. Walker is an Australian author, who loves her genre of gay romance. She loves writing and spends far too much time doing it, but wouldn't have it any other way.

She is many things: a mother, a wife, a sister, a writer. She has pretty, pretty boys who live in her head, who don't let her sleep at night unless she gives them life with words.

She likes it when they do dirty, dirty things... but likes it even more when they fall in love.

She used to think having people in her head talking to her was weird, until one day she happened across other writers who told her it was normal.

She's been writing ever since...

ALSO BY N.R. WALKER

The Spencer Cohen Series, Book One

The Spencer Cohen Series, Book Two

The Spencer Cohen Series, Book Three

The Spencer Cohen Series, Yanni's Story

Blood & Milk

The Weight Of It All

A Very Henry Christmas (The Weight of It All 1.5)

Perfect Catch

Switched

Imago

Imagines

Red Dirt Heart Imago

On Davis Row

Finders Keepers

Evolved

Galaxies and Oceans

Private Charter

Nova Praetorian

A Soldier's Wish

Titles in Audio:

Cronin's Key

Cronin's Key II

Cronin's Key III

Red Dirt Heart

Red Dirt Heart 2

Red Dirt Heart 3

Red Dirt Heart 4

The Weight Of It All

Switched

Point of No Return

Breaking Point

Starting Point

Spencer Cohen Book One

Spencer Cohen Book Two

Spencer Cohen Book Three

Yanni's Story

On Davis Row

Evolved

Free Reads:

Sixty Five Hours

Learning to Feel

His Grandfather's Watch (And The Story of Billy and Hale)

The Twelfth of Never (Blind Faith 3.5)

Twelve Days of Christmas (Sixty Five Hours Christmas)

Best of Both Worlds

Translated Titles:

Fiducia Cieca (Italian translation of Blind Faith)

Attraverso Questi Occhi (Italian translation of Through These Eyes)

Preso alla Sprovvista (Italian translation of Blindside)

Il giorno del Mai (Italian translation of Blind Faith 3.5)

Cuore di Terra Rossa (Italian translation of Red Dirt Heart)

Cuore di Terra Rossa 2 (Italian translation of Red Dirt Heart 2)

Cuore di Terra Rossa 3 (Italian translation of Red Dirt Heart 3)

Cuore di Terra Rossa 4 (Italian translation of Red Dirt Heart 4)

Intervento di Retrofit (Italian translation of Elements of Retrofit)

A Chiare Linee (Italian translation of Clarity of Lines)

Senso d'appartenenza (Italian translation of Sense of Place)

Confiance Aveugle (French translation of Blind Faith)

A travers ces yeux: Confiance Aveugle 2 (French translation of Through These Eyes)

Aveugle: Confiance Aveugle 3 (French translation of Blindside)

À Jamais (French translation of Blind Faith 3.5)

Cronin's Key (French translation)

Cronin's Key II (French translation)

Au Coeur de Sutton Station (French translation of Red Dirt Heart)

Partir ou rester (French translation of Red Dirt Heart 2)

Faire Face (French translation of Red Dirt Heart 3)

Trouver sa Place (French translation of Red Dirt Heart 4)

Un noël à Sutton Station (French translation of Red Dirt Heart Christmas)

Red Dirt Heart - L'intégrale (French translation of Red Dirt Series book set)

Rote Erde (German translation of Red Dirt Heart)

Rote Erde 2 (German translation of Red Dirt Heart 2)

Ein kleines bisschen Versuchung (German translation of The Weight of It All)

Ein kleines bisschen für immer (German translation of The Weight of It All Christmas)

65 Hours (Thai translation of Sixty Five Hours

CPSIA information can be obtained
at www.ICGtesting.com
Printed in the USA
LVHW040620121020
668550LV00003B/246